Books by Graham Swift

THE SWEET-SHOP OWNER
SHUTTLECOCK
LEARNING TO SWIM
WATERLAND
OUT OF THIS WORLD

Out
OF THIS
World

GRAHAM SWIFT

Poseidon Press

NEW YORK   LONDON   TORONTO   SYDNEY   TOKYO

Poseidon Press
Simon & Schuster Building
Rockefeller Center
1230 Avenue of the Americas
New York, New York 10020

Originally published in Great Britain by the Penguin Group

POSEIDON PRESS is a registered trademark
of Simon & Schuster Inc.

POSEIDON PRESS colophon is a trademark
of Simon & Schuster Inc.

Manufactured in the United States of America

10 9 8 7 6 5 4 3 2 1

Library of Congress Cataloging-in-Publication Data

Swift, Graham, date.
   Out of this world.
   I. Title.

PR6069.W4709   1988   823'.914   88-17799

ISBN 0-671-65827-1

*The quotation on p. 52 from the song "Summertime" (composer: George Gershwin; author: DuBose Heyward; copyright 1935 by Gershwin Publ. Corp.) is reproduced by permission of Chappell Music Ltd.

FOR CANDICE

What the eye sees not, the heart rues not.

APRIL 1982

HARRY

——

I remember, in '69, three years before he died, when I was
home for a brief while in the summer, how we sat up together
all night watching those first moon-men take their first, shy
steps on the moon. I didn't think he'd care. Didn't think he'd
give a toss about that old dream come true. But he watched
those pictures as if it were all some solemn duty he couldn't
neglect. He'd turned seventy that previous winter. Talked about
'three score and ten'. And some time that night he leant across
to chink his whisky glass against mine and said, without sarcasm, 'I've lived to see men land on the moon.' As if he truly
found the fact momentous, as if he were proud that his life
spanned the full, galloping gamut of the twentieth century.

We were close that night. We talked. We talked! He said it
was time he was getting out. Getting out of Irving's way. And
he'd never said it like that before, as if it wasn't just some tired,
insincere prevarication but he really wanted his release. It
wasn't home any more, he said, it was headquarters. And it was
true, he'd had barbed wire strung from angled posts all along
the boundary wall, new alarms wired up. Though that was
nothing to what Irving would have in three years' time. To
what Irving was now. And those jokes I used to make – the

11

'Arsenal', the 'Fortress' – they weren't jokes I could make any more. Though I'd never exactly meant them to be funny.

Not home. 'Headquarters'. He was going in less and less to the office. Getting 'security-conscious'. After a whisky or two more he started to drop hints about how they were moving into serious stuff. Not just the regular old range but heavy systems. The word was 'systems' now. Missile components. Ground-to-air. Air-to-air. I said: So was there a scale in these things?

That year, like the one before, was all Vietnam. That spring I'd been at Dau Tieng and around Tay Ninh and in the A Shau, where the war had reached the inane pitch of being fought to prove that a war was being fought and so keep the Paris negotiators on their toes. And I was just back again, only three weeks, from Saigon, and nothing was real. The moon over English elm trees wasn't real, and men walking on the moon was, in the language of those days, just far out, far out. But I was used to that feeling. Coming back to 'normal' places, 'home' even. Used to that feeling by then. Could bargain with it, parley with it, mollify it with whisky. That previous year, though I could scarcely believe it, I'd turned fifty. Fifty to his seventy. So we both had a big number to celebrate. A lean, stringy sort of fifty. Adrenalized and tensed. So the confused, angry kids, denimed and beaded, I photographed in Lincoln Park, Chicago, as inside the convention hall they sang 'Happy Days Are Here Again', didn't even think of me as another generation. They said: That's Harry Beech – he's been *out there*. Some of them actually wanted my autograph.

And 'out there' I wasn't old. ('Hey man, did you say "fifty" – like *five-o?*') Because out there everyone was old.

A gaunt, taut face in the mirror, which didn't look like any age. With eyes that I knew stared more and blinked less than they should. And a neat white zip of a scar above my left jaw where a piece of flying something caught me in Stanleyville. My one, negligible wound in the cause of. I didn't feel a thing.

Just the gush of blood in my mouth, and the thought: O my God, I'm coughing this *up*. Then the discovery I could poke my tongue through my cheek.

All Vietnam. And, of course, the Apollo missions. Which were the other side, the shiny side of the coin. The bright side of the moon. And maybe they weren't so different, just part of the same programme, those moon-men, mission-controlled men in their absurd outfits, and the marines I photographed out on patrol, with their helmets and flak-jackets and grenades and antennae. M-16s, M-60s, M-79s. Just walking hardware too. Lunatic zones. 'The World', back home. The space-suits which didn't show if there was a real man inside. The body-bags lined up for the choppers to come in.

We watched them clamber out of the module. There was Armstrong's famous message to mankind. Which didn't work, because you knew it was rehearsed and the cameras were on him, cameras that didn't even have a human eye behind them. Then Nixon's voice, crackling across space.

The first rule of photography: that you must catch things unawares. That the camera doesn't manufacture. But that night was the first time perhaps that I thought: No, times have changed since then. The camera first, then the event. The whole world is waiting just to get turned into film. And not just the world but the goddam moon as well.

First Armstrong, then Aldrin, bobbing over the lunar dust. Just for one wild moment you thought: They are going to start jumping and bouncing for sheer joy. They are going to start leaping and cavorting, in that gravity-less freedom, in those clown suits, for sheer, delirious amazement that they are there on the surface of the moon.

They say that afterwards, after they got back to earth, some of those astronauts, some of those Apollo pioneers got religion. Those robot-men, clones of NASA technology, became crew-cut mystics, speaking at meetings about the View from Up

13

There. The irony of it. That we should have spent centuries shedding superstition and actually evolving the means that would get us up into Heaven. Only to discover that, all along, *He* was there first.

That was not part of the programme. Played down in the post-mission publicity. But the moon-dust, the rocks, the samples: people queued up for hours just to look at some dust and some rocks. And the pictures. The earth from the moon. The ultimate photo. All of it, the whole of it, everything. Hanging in the black velvet of space. I wish I could have taken that photo. Stopped there.

For some reason we were closer than we'd ever been. It was our closeness that mattered, more than the men on the distant moon. We stopped watching the TV. It gets boring after a while – moon-walking, rock collecting, puppets bouncing on dust. We opened the French windows and went out on to the terrace. I suppose all over the world people must have done that that night: left their TV sets and gone to stare at the sky. We stood on the terrace in the gathering light. There was an expression on his face as if he, too, didn't know what was real or what wasn't. I remember I took his arm. I mean, I was standing on his right side, his wrong side, and I put my hand on the arm that wasn't his arm. On his artificial arm. And just a little while after that – it had taken him till he was seventy and I was fifty – he told me how it had happened.

SOPHIE

——

I guess I belong to the new world now, Doctor K. You see – I even say, 'I guess'. Save that it isn't the new world. That old idea was always just a dream, wasn't it, a come-on, a sales pitch? The land of escape, the land of sanctuary. New worlds for old. And I'm not blind to the fact that what Joe sells every day in his Sixth Avenue office – what keeps us here in the land of the free – is just the same dream only in reverse: golden memories of the Old World. Thatched cottages and stately homes. Patchwork scenery. Sweet, green visions. Oh to be in England now that – (Now, so it seems, they are off to fight the Argentines.)

Yet it was he who brought us here, refugees of a kind, to the new world. Though it was not exactly, then, in '72, the Promised Land, and we were not exactly huddled in steerage with our bundled belongings. There was Grandad's money, for a start. Though Joe would still maintain that it was his own gallant, provident decision. As if he'd *known*. To take us 'away from it all'. But away-from-it-all is such a shifting, strange, elusive place. There isn't a point in the world where you can get away from the world, not any more, is there?

And it was really my decision. I could have said, that day, to

Grandad: Yes, I want it. I really do. Yes. And Joe will take the job, a job he doesn't even understand. For my sake. The weather-cocks, the yew trees, the orchard walls. The whole damn fragile illusion.

But now he keeps the illusion that he brought us here. Away from it all. And I know what he would answer if someone were to say to him that he's in the business of dreams. 'Sure. But better to sell dreams than – Better, any time, to sell pleasure, even pre-packaged, glossy-brochured pleasure, than – '

You know what first struck me about New York? (I mean, after that first impression that lasts about two days, that it is all some vast hallucination.) That all these clean, hard, soaring, futuristic lines were mixed up with something crumbling, blighted, decomposed. As if the skyscrapers had to sprout out of some fertile rot. But sweetness and innocence were never really the ticket, were they? If you want them, go walk in some English meadow. And now that's just what they're paying, a thousand bucks a time, to do.

The land of cancelled memories. The land without a past. For you too, Doctor K? Some mishap in middle Europe, some-where along the line? Refugee makes good? But – I forget – you don't talk. You just listen. I'm the one who has to do the talking.

The land of amnesty. And the land of the gun. Do you remember (our little affair had only just started), we were walking in the Park, you in your tweed coat and hundred-and-fifty-dollar shoes, and me with a winter flush in my cheeks? And I said, just like a smart-ass student to her sugar-daddy professor, no, just like a pert little daughter to her daddy, no, just like a precocious young belle to her old-fashioned gentle-manly beau: This much-debated violence of American life, it was hardly surprising, was it? Since America was made out of bottled-up bad memories, by people on the run. And you narrowed your eyes and, with a little touch of mimic-Bronx, said, 'Say, who's the analyst round here?' And then, straightening your gloves: 'And spare me the collective unconscious, please. One mind at a time is plenty.' You bought me tea at the Tavern. I thought: If you want to propose something – something strictly unprofessional – now is your chance.

Not away from it all. Joe wouldn't have understood how I felt safe, here in this unsafe country, immune in this perilous city. Me, a sweet English (half-Greek) rose in wicked, wild New York. There's a sort of comfort, a sort of security, isn't there, in the absence of disguise, in knowing the way things really are? The land of violence, the land of the gun. You know, the ever-so-gentle and peaceable English have this far-fetched notion of America as the place where to settle their differences – to eliminate red indians, outlaws, negroes, presidents, protesting citizens, rival mobsters and business competitors – they pull out a gun and shoot.

So why this terror of a *toy* gun, Sophie?

I'm trying to *tell* you, for JESUS CHRISSAKE!

Dear Doctor Klein. The things I haven't told you. The things I never told you. When we first came here in '72, I didn't know anything about anything. I was just a dumb young wife ('Not dumb, Sophie, never dumb'), pregnant for the first – and I guess the only – time, not even suspecting she was going to have twins, waking up in a new world. I don't know if I felt at once, this is where I belong now, or whether it was years before anything touched me. I thought: It's ugly – so it's beautiful. It's threatening, that's okay. I'd rather danger jumped out at you when you half expect it, than suddenly explode from green lawns and mellow brick walls.

Then the boys were born and Joe started to make good and we got this place here in Brooklyn. For a while there was this succession of men coming to fix the plumbing, the heating, to fit the kitchen. I did the proper things then – kept the chain on the door, asked to see their cards. If you put up barriers, you

17

show you are vulnerable. One of them – his name was Georgiades, Nick Georgiades – said, 'You new to New York?' So I
must have still looked like some dazed outsider. I said yes. He
looked at me. 'From Europe?' I love the way Americans say
'Europe', as if little countries like England or Germany don't
count. 'I bin to Europe,' he said. I thought: He's big and ugly.
'They got a lot of pretty things over there. But I prefer New
York. You know what I think?' He was fixing some pipe under
the sink, half lying on the floor, but looking at me as he tugged
with a spanner. 'Europe is like a broad all dressed up. You
don't know what's underneath. But New York is like a broad
without any clothes. She may not be a princess, but she's naked
and she sure as hell is real.'

I can tell you anything, can't I, I can tell you everything –
isn't that the idea? Like the doctor I'd let peer up my vagina, I
let you peer into my mind. You could be having a voyeur's
field-day, but it's okay, because it's your job, you've got quali-
fications.

I said, 'So you're not Greek then?' He thought this was
funny. 'Just a name – one of my fathers was Greek.' He
laughed. I said my mother was Greek, and stood nearer so he
could look at my legs. He said, 'Uhuh. Uhuh. Old man at
work?'

He got up, put the spanner down, and I can't remember
making up my mind to do it, but I put my hand on his cock,
hard as a pistol, and he hitched up my skirt, right here in this
kitchen, with his hands greasy, with the twins upstairs sleeping,
and I said, 'C'mon! C'mon fuck me, fuck me good, you great
hog!' And after that I was no longer a new-world virgin.

HARRY

——

Every year I still go to see Marion Evans. She doesn't lose her
memory. We drive up to Epsom Downs usually, if the weather
is fine. She brings a thermos. She's never told me and I've
never asked what she did with Ray's ashes, but I have a hunch
she just scattered them up there, early one Sunday morning.
And I have a hunch too that what crossed my mind must surely
have crossed hers: that there must have been some of Dad's
ashes mixed up with Ray's. So it's a kind of double observance
when we drive up there.

We park the car, wind the windows down, look out over the
race-course. She pours tea from the thermos. I ask after her
married son and daughter and her grandchildren, and she gives
me matter-of-fact accounts. She asks do I hear from Sophie?
And I say, Yes, she's fine. And the twins? Fine. Which is a lie
on at least two counts. Because according to Joe's latest bulletin
(no, Mrs Evans, Sophie doesn't write and I don't write to her,
and I've never seen my grandchildren), Sophie isn't exactly fine
at all.

I can tell from her voice and the look in her eye that neither
she nor any of her family has ever got over that explosion ten
years ago. There's still this feeling that Ray was to blame

19

somehow. He failed in his duty, should have looked under the back seat as well as the bonnet and in the boot and underneath. Just *because* he was a victim, he must be implicated in some way. And so must they. They will never get back again into that safe, simple, well-defined world in which the head of the family was a trusted chauffeur, seventeen years with Dad, and a shrewd follower of horses.

She always says I should take up 'the photography' again. People ought to know about 'those things'. They ought to know. I say, Someone else can take the pictures now. And maybe, these days, people have seen it all anyway. I look away as I say this. Because eleven, twelve years ago I know she'd have thought differently. She'd have thought what Ray thought of me. Which, though he always gave me the respectful salute and the time of day, was that I was an oddball, a black sheep. Even when I'd made a name for myself. He took Dad's side. Naturally.

'Besides, I'm getting too old for running around any more.'

(As if it were a sport.)

'You're the youngest sixty-four-year-old I know.'

And how is the cottage? she asks. And I feel embarrassed again, because this would be the fifth or sixth year of Ray's retirement. It's fine, I say. It must be nice that, she says, a cottage in the country. And do I still go up in the planes? Yes, I still go up in the planes.

'There you are, you see, at your age.'

And never once, in nine visits, has she voiced any outrage, any fury, that Dad got the hero's treatment, the front-page funeral, and Ray was just the poignant sub-plot. 'The loyalty that inspired loyalty . . .'

We sip our tea, gazing at the white grandstand. The car we sit in has been scrupulously scoured for any sign or scent of a feminine presence. Jenny's comb, long hairs in its teeth, peeping from under the passenger seat. I wouldn't dare and

20

couldn't bear, on this of all days (though, God knows, she'll have to know some time), to tell Marion that, actually, I am happy. That in spite of everything (and at my age!) I am actually –

I swallow my tea carefully, like a guilty husband. You won't blame me, Mrs Evans, laugh at me? Refuse to meet me again?

On Epsom Downs people exercise dogs, and fly kites and model aeroplanes. And there are the horses. He liked horses. Picked the winners. Groomed my daughter's horse. Chauffeur and stableman.

Marion used to invite me to stay for dinner. But after the third or fourth time, because I always said no, she stopped asking. I drive her home. Marion is sixty-eight, but I always feel vastly her junior. Her semi-detached in Epsom is trim, immaculate, lovingly cared for. I've looked at many things that are difficult to look at, but when I leave and she stands at the front door, brushing hair from her forehead, upright, unsmiling, it breaks me up. My chest starts to heave.

I go to Dad's grave too. It's on the way back, and I deliberately leave it till the evening, so I won't stumble upon anyone. Upon Frank perhaps, piously making a personal visit. The Surrey churchyard, the lych-gate and yew trees always depress me. What did they put in that coffin? And I'm troubled by the litter of tributes that, even after ten years, festoons the grave itself. The biggest wreath, as always, from BMC. Another from his regiment (that was over sixty years ago). Others from the hospitals in Guildford and Chiswick (left them several grand apiece), from old colleagues and pals in the M.O.D. and the Royal Ordnance. One, with a fulsome message, from the Conservative Club. Flowers from the parish and local big-wigs. Even an offering from the primary school.

The blast was big enough. The police concluded that Ray must have shut the passenger door, got back into the driver's

21

seat and shut his own door before the bomb, a crude device operated by simple pressure, was detonated by some shifting of Dad in his seat. Death instantaneous. The shut doors acted to contain but also to intensify the shock. The explosion not only totally destroyed a Daimler New Sovereign but gouged a crater in the gravel drive, shattered every window in the front of the house – in several cases damaging irreparably the Queen Anne window frames and lacerating the furniture inside – gashed the brickwork and stucco, blew in the front door, and deafened the other three occupants of the house on that Monday morning: namely Mrs Keane, Dad's housekeeper, Sophie Beech, his grand-daughter, and Harry, his son.

I stand for a few moments by the grave, hands in my pockets. I won't be tricked. How do we make such decisions? How do we decide that one life matters and another doesn't? How do we solemnize one death and ignore a thousand others?

Usually, after leaving the churchyard, I take the minor road past Hyfield. Past the Six Bells pub, the cricket ground. I slow down where the road skirts the garden wall and the entrance. There are solid metal gates, replacing the former wrought-iron ones which used to give a glimpse of the house. The dog warnings. And perched in discreet but strategic places above the wall and the barbed wire, the cameras.

You could say I put you there, Frank. So if you feel like a prisoner too, you can blame me. But perhaps it doesn't feel like a prison, perhaps it just feels like a well-guarded home. And it's where you always wanted to be. For thirty-odd years you were my alibi, my decoy. You were part of my scheme, though you probably assumed – I know you assumed – I was part of yours. No, unlike Ray Evans, I was never the innocent victim. No saint. Just your usual bastard. A bad father and, some people would say, a bad son. But I was a good husband for seven years to Anna. And if she were still alive I might be sitting where you are now. I might never have become Harry Beech the photo-journalist, the

22

ex-photo-journalist. I might have done all that: become what
you are, what Dad was. Just for her sake. Just for simple, selfish
love's old sake. So perhaps you should thank me.

SOPHIE

But doesn't it get to you, Doctor K? Other people's minds. Other people's mess. How do you feel at the end of the day? Kind of dirty? Kind of tainted? Or what do you do? Put your notes away. Stretch your arms and crack your knuckles. Cut off. Fix a drink maybe and make some calls. Look out from your window over the chasm of 59th Street.

Do you think of me when I'm not with you? Do you have thoughts?

Okay, so, like you tell me, I'm not so dumb. I know I'm just one of many. I'm 'File under "C" for Carmichael'. Not 'S' for Sophie. This fast, promiscuous life you lead. A gigolo of the psyche. Rule number one: make each one of them feel special, make each one of them feel they're the only one. (A subtle and mature gigolo, with silvery temples and a dry, seasoned style. Old enough to be my –)

'Let's talk about you, Doctor K.'

'Oh no, Sophie.'

A shake of the head, a wag of the finger, a patient smile. Like a gentle, kindly schoolmaster. Rule number two. 'You do the talking, Sophie. I'll ask the questions. Yes, it's a tough deal, isn't it? You have the work to do, and I'm the one who gets paid. But isn't it nice to have someone who'll listen, who's there to listen? You don't need to know about me. Just think of me as a hired listener. Just think of me as two ears and a notebook.'

I bet you give the same patter to all the girls. Make the same wisecracks. I bet you take them all for walks in the Park, buy them tea and let them slip their hands through your own well-crooked, well-tailored arm.

'If Central Park is the Garden of Eden, Sophie, it is surrounded by the Fall of Manhattan.'

(A leather-bound notebook. And two very cute ears.)

What do I know about you? You're married? Have kids? You're divorced? You like little girls? Or muscular young men?

But maybe you're right. If I knew only a little more about you maybe I wouldn't think of you as Mister Calm, as Mister Wonderful, as Mister Well-adjusted and Oh-so-civilized, gazing out with your Martini, over this most anxious city on earth.

Look at these men in their fifties, jogging, red-faced, round the Park. They look so ill, they look so desperate. They look so in need of punishment and penance. Not you, eh?

You have it both ways. You see and you're not seen. You take a good long peek, but you remain immune.

(But don't you think about me, just a bit?)

What you never know will never hurt you. Is that it? And what you know, you can't ever unknow. Though you can have a damn good try. But when you try to remember what it was like long, long ago, you can't ever do it without knowing the things you were going to find out later, without seeing yourself like those people in dreams you try to call out to and warn, and who never hear you.

Poor Tim, poor Paul. My poor dear darlings.

We should turn round now? Stroll back? It's nearly four o'clock. Hey, if we're lucky we'll catch the chimes and the dancing animals on the Delacorte Clock.

26

And you know what scares me more than anything? That it won't make any difference, that it won't have any effect. Look at them, watching the TV, while I watch them, a bringer of bad news, poised in the doorway. Cookies and milk. My angels. They're sipping in the pictures. Lapping up the universe. Who needs a mother any more?

You know, when Mum died I just didn't believe it. Can you remember what it was like (okay, so *I'm* asking questions) before you really knew about death? I was five years old. She went off one day and didn't come back. But I always thought she would have to come back some day. I don't know how long it was before I really understood she was never coming back. And, you know, when Harry started going off for months on end, when he left me and Grandad and went off to do his thing with the world, to be where it was happening, I used to think that what he was doing was looking for Mum. And I used to blame him – have you got this, are you writing this down? – because he never found her.

HARRY

———

I was born on March 27th, 1918, and I never knew my mother, because on that same day (can it have been so long ago?), at the very same hour, she died.

They say that if there has to be a choice, it is the doctor's duty to save the child before the mother. In certain situations life is tradeable, expendable. It is the field surgeon's duty to repair the lightly wounded before the probable fatalities. Had the choice been my father's, I know, without doubt, how he would have chosen. He would have wanted my mother to live. I don't blame him. The choice would have been only natural. He would never have known or even seen me, but he would have seen my mother again. But at the time of my birth my father was not in a position to choose. He was far away, in another country and, as it happened, in another of those situations where life was expendable.

He made, all the same, another choice. (He made two choices, though half a century went by before I knew about that other, big choice, that failed.) He might have loved me with a double, a compound love. He chose instead to blame me, to see me as the instrument of his wife's death. And had I known this as a small boy, had I known it even as an ignorant baby, I think I would have gladly affirmed that I wished I could have made that very first choice in my mother's favour, and so restored her to him. A great many things would then have been different (though I would have known nothing about them). But I was not in a position of choice.

On my birthday he would hand over some present and I would receive it like an emblem of guilt. In this way he once gave me a camera. Then he would disappear for the rest of the day.

It took me years to work all this out. But I never worked off the blame. I never thought, though I learned to scorn him just as he scorned me, that I deserved anything other than a father who, if he inspired esteem and even fondness in others, was as tender to me as a statue. Even when he held Sophie for the very first time – we had been father and son then for *thirty* years – and I saw him smile and his eyes moisten, I didn't think: You old bastard, so now you can afford to relent, to be reconciled, to let it all come out. I thought: Thank God, I have made Dad melt. I have paid my debt.

And I truly believe he was glad when Anna died. Because it was only then that we started, really, to be friends. As if I hadn't paid the debt, not till then. Oh no, not in full.

You too, Harry. Now you know what it's like.

I can see them now, sitting on the wicker chairs on the lawn at Hyfield. He is making her laugh and she is making him laugh. She used to call him the 'perfect gentleman'. She used to call him in Greek her '*palikári*'. It is, let's say, August '53, and she has only three months to live. I am walking across the lawn from the house and seeing all this as if I have just chanced, inadvertently, on the scene. When I appear she checks her laughter momentarily, as if I am intruding. Sophie is lying, stomach down, on the grass, looking at a book. She is five years old. Anna is wearing a sky-blue summer dress with thin shoulder-straps. She carries on laughing and Sophie looks up

30

and smiles, and I can tell that she knows her mother is beautiful.

When Sophie was born a strange thing happened. Though it's not really strange at all. It must be one of the commonest experiences. But I had never imagined what it was like to be a parent. I became afraid. I had never reckoned on this fear. In the most easy and safe domains of playtime, bathtime and bedtime, I became afraid. I was always thinking that at any moment, because of some slight inattention, she might die – fall, suffocate, be knocked down, her little body smashed. And once indeed it very nearly happened, she nearly drowned.

I still maintain she was drowning.

I never expected such fear and such terrible, crushing love. When I held her in my arms I never wanted to let go, because of the risks. It was as though only my arms were protecting Sophie from the world. Or rather that I was making a separate world within the circle of my arms. When I pressed my face against the white blankets she was wrapped in I would remember the valley in Switzerland where Anna and I spent our hasty honeymoon, the pure air, the white drapery of the mountains which only two years before had been a real curtain against the world. *'Meine Frau ist Griechin.'* *'Ja, eine Göttin, nein?'* And I would think, on our weekend visits to Hyfield: What does it matter? What does it matter? I will say the word to Dad, and get the slap on the back that has been thwarted for thirty years, the stiff drink thrust into my hand. And who, anyway, can say they have a choice over their life?

Okay, Dad, count me in.

To protect Sophie. For Sophie's sake. And Anna's.

It was absurd, that terror that Sophie might die. In Nuremberg, where I met Anna, they were itemizing the deaths of millions. As if she were especially prone, as if she alone were up on some thin high-wire of mortality. But how often did I utter that familiar, silent prayer: If someone must die, let it be

31

somebody else, let it be some other little girl, not Sophie. Or even: If someone must die, let it be me, not her.

Life is tradeable, expendable.

And the irony was that it wasn't Sophie who died. It was Anna. She died on Mount Olympus. Ridiculous or sublime? And in her case there was never a choice between mother and child. Because when she died she was six weeks pregnant.

She was going to see her Uncle Spiro, whom she hadn't seen for seven years and who was dying in a hospital in Salonika. But she died before he did, because her plane hit a thunderstorm, and then a mountain.

And I never wished – So help me, I never, not for one moment, wished –

SOPHIE

'Why do you call him "Harry"?'

'Because that's his name. Harry Beech. Haven't you heard of Harry Beech? The famous Harry Beech? Because I stopped calling him "Dad". Because the last time I saw him I called him "Harry" for the first time to his face. Now when I think of him, it's "Harry".'

'You think of him much?'

'No. And I don't think much of him! Ha ha!'

'When was that – the last time you saw him?'

'May 3rd, 1972. About six o'clock in the afternoon.'

'How so exact?'

'Because that was the day they put Grandad in the ground.'

'Put him in the ground?'

'You bury a body. There were only little bits of Grandad.'

'Sophie, I'd like you to tell me something. When you think of your father what's the first word that comes into your head?'

'Oh good, so we're going to play games! So shrinks really ask those questions? Let me see now. How about: "Stranger"? No? Too neat? Did I have too much time to think? How about: "Cunt"?'

33

'And when you think of your grandfather?'

'"Home". "Little bits". Ask me another.'

'Can you picture him?'

'Grandad?'

'Your father.'

'Harry.'

'Okay – Harry.'

'This couch is really comfy. Do you get your men clients to lie on it, or just the women?'

'Can you picture him?'

'You mean, what he looks like? I don't know. I guess he's much the same. He was always – what's the word? – well-preserved.'

'But you don't think of him much?'

'Out of sight, out of mind. Isn't that the way?'

'I don't know, Sophie, you tell me. Do you know what he's doing now?'

'Nope. He's not a news photographer, that's for sure.'

'Do you love your father, Sophie?'

'Fuck you.'

'So, how come he stopped being a photographer?'

HARRY

——

Michael comes to pick us up at six. It's the light. Long shadows.
You need the morning or the evening light. When he arrives he
still gives his policeman's rat-a-tat knock and when he ducks
through the cottage door he does so with the slightly guarded
air of the solidly married man entering a newly built love-nest.
He winks at Jenny as he might at the comely girl-friend of one
of his teenage sons. Six weeks ago I phoned him and said, Can
we take four in the plane? – Jenny wants to come too. He said,
Okay, no problem, no extra charge. He said, Would she meet
us there? And I said, No, she'd be here at the cottage, with me.
There was a pause. Then he said, Okay.

We are dressed and waiting, Jenny in her blue sweater and
jeans. She sits at the table while I make toast. She holds her mug
in both hands, elbows on the table, and dips her face towards it,
eyes peering at me over the rim. We haven't told anyone. Not yet.

We drive to the airfield. The hills of Wiltshire, smoky and
silvery in the early light, roll by. Rabbits sprint for cover as
we pass. And I know it's absurd, a descent into second
schoolboyhood – in a man of my age and (should I say it?)
experience – but I relish this feeling of the dawn mission: the
ride to the airfield, the nip in the air, the mugs of hot tea.

Jenny sits in the front with Michael. I sit in the back with the cameras. Michael is humanized, vitalized by machines. Seated at the controls of an aircraft, a car, he becomes natural, buoyant, fluent. Jenny and he are talking, chuckling, almost as if I am not there, and I don't listen to what they are saying. The back of Jenny's head, the curve of her cheek as she looks towards Michael, enthral me. When she turns fully to catch my glance and smile, secret pods of joy burst inside me.

There were jokes, of the usual kind, I suppose, between Michael and Peter about me and my 'assistant'. It went, perhaps, with my supposedly adventurous past. Unspoken estimations. So how many girls, Harry, in foreign cities, foreign beds? But I know and Michael knows it's not really like that. Both he and Peter are half in love with her themselves. And quite right too. She's beautiful. She's incredible. She's out of this world.

Peter is there before us, parking his yellow 2CV. Peter has the dignified title of Archaeological Consultant to the Southern Counties Commission on Ancient Monuments, and looks like an out-of-work actor. He himself admits that, as a financial proposition, there is not much difference between the aspiring actor and the aspiring archaeologist. But he is stage-struck on the Bronze Age and the Iron Age, on the hidden spectacle of the past. He is convinced that between ST880390 and ST960370 there is a whole network of undiscovered field systems. It depends on the light, the rainfall and the vegetation factor. But one day, from the air, they'll show.

This is the fourth of these flights. There will be others through the summer. Jenny doesn't come up in the plane any more. She was sick that first time she joined us, never having flown in a light aircraft before. But she insists on coming, nonetheless, to the airfield.

Michael goes to check over the Cessna. We go into the low building under the control tower where there is a small office that Derek, the ground control deputy, lets Jenny use while we are in the air. Derek's stock response to Jenny's presence is also a semi-paternal wink. While we circle over England, he will offer her further chapters from his life's story. Flying Dakotas in Malaya. His grown-up children in Australia. I don't know what Jenny tells him.

Jenny unpacks the cameras. Under the table I stroke her thigh. Peter looks studiously at his maps. He is shy and deferential with Jenny. I don't know if he'd rather she didn't appear at all for our morning sorties. I am sorry to have brought this disturbance, this distraction into his pure and devoted passion for the Bronze Age.

Peter pushes the map across and briefs me on our 'targets'. Under the table Jenny's hand finds my roaming hand and squeezes it.

I surfaced again – or rather, took to the air. And didn't entirely jettison my camera. In the autumn of '72 I sold a house and photographic studio (unused for six months) in Fulham and, having been used to travelling, as Dad would put it, 'to the ends of the earth', bought a cottage in a village, a few miles from Marlborough, with the ludicrously parochial name of Little Stover. (There is no Great Stover. Look on the map, you won't find it.) A retreat? An escape? An attack of rustic regression? Maybe. But Little Stover, which has no big brother, happens to be only five miles from one of the most centrally placed civil airfields in southern England. In 1973 I converted an attic into a dark-room and office, and (being not without some previous experience) set up shop as an aerial photographer.

We walk towards the Cessna. Large, still puddles in the tarmac reflect the lightening sky. The air is chilly and Jenny clutches my arm. I told her about Anna. How – So I know one

37

reason why she comes to the airfield. I tell her Michael's been flying for twenty-five years – five years with me – and never – And I've been in more planes and helicopters than I can remember, many of them military aircraft in the middle of war zones, and never – (Save once, out of Pleiku – though I didn't tell her this – when something like an airborne shunt engine hit our Huey, two, three times, unbelievably and maliciously, and I got the pilot's expression as he spewed blue language and took what he later called 'some evasive' ('Helicopter Pilot under Ground Fire, Central Highlands, 1966'), and it occurred to me that not for one moment, though my heart was bursting and my stomach was nowhere and my brain was saying, This time, *this* time – not for one moment was I actually scared.)

And I have always loved flying. Never (despite such moments) lost the magic of it. That release from the ground. Those cloud-oceans. Those light-shows, coming down at night into strange, spangled cities. If I had not been a photographer, I would have been a pilot. Would have put my name down for the moon.

And yet in sixty-four years I have never learnt to fly. Sometimes in our airborne jaunts over England – perhaps my present occupation is only an excuse for indulging my love of flying – Michael, against all the rules of common sense and civil aviation, offers me the controls. As if in some kind of challenge (that first time we went up together: suddenly puts me through a stomach-churning show of unannounced aerobatics. To prove what?). Or so he can say afterwards, like some stern father to a feckless son: When are you going to take some proper lessons?

We clamber into the cockpit. Jenny passes up the cameras. Gives me a brief, knowing look. Peter has a last-minute word with Michael. He is feeling good today about 880390 and 960370. The engine roars and Jenny steps back and throws a quick and generalized kiss, trying to make the gesture more casual than she means. We taxi down to the runway, turn, and

Michael opens the throttle. We speed back in the direction we have come and as we ascend over the apron and the tower, we see her wave, in that stubborn, clumsy way in which people wave when they cannot see if their wave is acknowledged. She is still holding a hand aloft as we bank to head south. And I could almost believe it, could almost be guilty of believing it: the rest of the world doesn't matter. The world revolves round that tinier and tinier figure, as it revolves round a cottage in a tiny village in Wiltshire, where she has taken up residence. That I am home, home.

SOPHIE

—

'It's the wrong name, isn't it? "Harry". "Harry" sounds like the reliable sort. An uncle, a best man, a loyal old flame.'

'And he's never written you in ten years?'

'No.'

'If you wrote him, would he write you? Is that how it is?'

'Don't know. Why don't you ask him?'

'I wish I could, Sophie. I wish he were right here now, so we could both ask him some questions. Do you wish that?'

'You've got nice hands. Neat. Has anyone ever told you that?'

'Supposing he were right here. Right now.'

'For fuck's sake.'

'You never miss him?'

'I miss Grandad.'

'But your grandfather's dead, and Harry's alive.'

'Spot on. You really have a way of cutting through the crap.'

'And Harry wasn't to blame for your grandfather's death.'

'No. Not to blame, no.'

'What do you mean, "not to blame"?'

'I mean it wasn't a case of blame.'

'What then?'

'Like I say, ask him.'

'You think it should have been your father who died somehow, not your grandfather?'

'Fuck.'

'Do you say "fuck" a lot at home, with Joe and the boys? Supposing I did ask him, what would he say?'

'He'd say, What is this, a fucking inquisition?'

'Okay, relax, Sophie. Relax. Touché. Truce. Let's take our time.'

'At eighty dollars an hour?'

'You want my economy deal? It's cheap, but there aren't any guarantees.'

'No, it's okay. I'll stick with deluxe. Joe pays.'

'What does Joe think of Harry?'

'I don't know if Joe thinks of Harry at all. Joe is good at forgetting.'

'He doesn't forget to pay.'

'Good.'

'Shall we have some coffee? Coffee time is free. So is the coffee.'

'Do you know, when you talk sometimes, you tug your ear?'

'It's a defence reflex, Sophie. According to the books, tugging your ear, scratching the back of your head, is a disguised defence reflex. You lift your arm to strike your enemy. What do you say?'

'I like it when you smile like that.'

'If he wrote you, would you write him?'

'Don't know.'

'But you've never written him?'

'No. I mean, yes. No.'

'What do you mean?'

'I mean I write him letters sometimes. In my head. I mean I don't put them on paper. I don't send them.'

'What sort of letters?'

42

'Just letters. Thoughts. You know.'

'Do you think he misses you?'

'Don't know.'

'But do you think he ever writes letters in his head, too – to you?'

'Don't know.'

HARRY

——

I still believe he fixed it. Some cunning string-pulling with his contacts in the Air Ministry. Though he never confessed it (so many unconfessed confessions! So many things buried away!). I still believe it was his doing that had me assigned, a fit, young, would-be flier, to a desk in Intelligence.

And yet he could have acted more ruthlessly, and with less trouble, if he'd wished. Could have foreclosed on my future. Insisted, since, undoubtedly, there was a busy time ahead, that I was needed at his side, and, since armaments were the reserved occupation *par excellence*, had me exempted from military service.

Though it's easy to see now that, in his position, he could hardly have put the duties of a son before those of a citizen. Amongst those heaps of papers he (involuntarily) left me (I never thought he would be the one for such careful documentation, for preserving the evidence) were the typescripts – annotated and underlined with red ink – of the speeches he made when he stood for Parliament in the Thirties. Now, when I read them, fifty years later, those heavy-handed phrases, those chastising and belligerent slogans prick at my eyes: 'manning the defences', 'the sleeping lion', 'moral re-armament'

– by which he meant, precisely, material re-armament. That was '35. The timing was just out. But the stance, the rhetoric (my God, I never went to hear him on the hustings) would be remembered later. Not least in those panegyrics after his death.

Right-hand man! My right-hand man, he would say. A dubious and all too blatant joke from a man with only one arm. I'll never know what the real motive was. Some absurd, implausible, residual dream? That it might all come right and good – Beech and Son, the two of us in tandem, the greater glory of BMC. For which he was prepared to wait and pay and bribe. My expensive and lengthy upbringing (Winchester, Oxford): a long-term investment in my filial conscience.

Or just a punishment? Just a kind of revenge?

'. . . You appear, Beech, to be a highly educated young man. It seems what we could most use from you are your brains . . .'

'. . . And we understand, Beech, that you are interested in photography . . .'

He laughed when I told him I had opted for the R.A.F. The rough, gravelly laugh of the former infantry officer. He laughed even more scoffingly (triumphantly?) when he learnt the result of my Board – that I was made of too precious stuff, so it seemed, to be flung into the skies. He never ceased to remind me that if, after all, mine was to be a non-combatant's role, I might as well have chosen to come in with him. That though, no doubt, I would have been worked off my feet, I would have been better off and better rewarded than in some 'wretched hut' in Lincolnshire. Perhaps – I can't recall it now – there was the tiniest, barely detectable flaw in this mockery, the tiniest, stubborn note of gratitude. I don't think I wanted to be a hero, a charioteer of the skies. My father was a hero. I didn't worship my father. But I had wanted to fly.

And yet I saw the war from the air. Since the officers of the Commissioning Board, in their obtuse or ironic wisdom, took literally my professed interest in photography. And the 'hut' in

Lincolnshire – in reality a small country house not unreminiscent of Hyfield – was given over to the analysis of aerial photographs.

I looked down with a privilege no pilot ever had on target after target. Before and after. I became routinely familiar with the geography of western Europe. At first a motley geography of steel works, dockyards, power stations, refineries, railways, then a geography (rapidly altering, diminishing) of cities. Hamburg, Bremen, Cologne, Essen, Düsseldorf, Berlin . . . I learnt to distinguish the marks of destruction – the massive ruptures of 4,000-pounders from the blisters of 1,000-pounders and the mere pock-marks of 250-pound clusters – and to translate these two-dimensional images, which were the records of three-dimensional facts, into one-dimensional formulae – tonnage dropped as against acreage devastated, acreage destroyed as against acreage attacked (the tallies never included 'people', 'homes') – while someone in the hierarchical clouds above me refined these figures into the ethereal concept known as 'the progress of operations'.

And as operations progressed, the statistics grew larger, the images more other-worldly, more crater-ridden, more lunar.

Frank Irving came to 'the Manor', as we called it, in the summer of '44. I was delegated to show him the ropes. He and I were two of the youngest on a staff dominated by men over forty. When I think of Frank, even now, I still think of Lincolnshire in the war. Of the broad, grassy Lincolnshire countryside, of draughty Lincolnshire pubs, and the strange stigma and exclusion of being junior Intelligence officers in a region littered with airfields and serving airmen. I think of the saloon bar of the Crown Hotel in Grantham, where there is a dearth of female company, let alone unattached female company, and where Frank, on his fifth pint and in fluent voice, is announcing the voluptuous procession that is shortly to enter through the amazed hotel portals: Hayworth, Lake, Grable, Lamour . . .

He arrived with a limp in his left leg (two fractures and a damaged tendon), the result of a motor-cycle accident that occurred before he had even begun his pilot's training. The story he told the Ladies of Lincolnshire (for we had our moments) was that he was shot down in his Spit back in '42 – hence the wretched desk job. While the story he conferred on me was a legendary and invisible head wound. Marvellous what these surgeons can do now. My friend Harry here – you won't believe it: totally blind in one eye.

False pretences. Of more than one kind? Did I intend it from the very beginning?

That summer, during fine weather, as the bombings intensified, we would sometimes be attached to the airfields themselves, working at all hours to monitor the raids and keep the crews effectively briefed. One hot July afternoon we were watching the tenders lumbering out to fill the bellies of the Lancs, and I said to him: 'Do you know who makes those bombs?'

He looked puzzled.

I said, 'My father.'

He looked puzzled still.

'You've heard of Beech Munitions? Robert Beech? BMC? Cannon balls by appointment . . .'

I think what he said then, and what he'd say still, though in a hundred subtle ways, was: 'Somebody has to make them.' But his eyes lost their puzzled look and after that day they acquired an ever-alert expression. Some weeks later when we both had three-day passes I asked him if he'd like to visit Hyfield. And I might have guessed that his eyes would become even more alert as we drove through the gates. As I might have known (had I wished it?) that Dad, tired and irascible as he was looking, would take a shine to him, would be the soul of affability, would take advantage of the situation to knock volleys into the air I had no way of returning.

'Now Harry will tell you ... Now when Harry takes over ...'

I pretended to be nonplussed.

That must have been in the early autumn of '44, after the liberation of Paris and before they sent me on that sudden photography course. They had decided by then that the war would be over before long and it was thus a historical phenomenon worthy of documentation. And my gauche enthusiasm back in '39 must have stuck on my file. I was sent to London where I was taught the parts and use of a camera in much the same manner as rifle drill. Then I was sent back to Lincolnshire, with equipment, a special pass and papers that would oblige senior and fellow officers to give me assistance, and told to get some pictures.

As if they might have said: You know, atmosphere, action, human drama stuff. Editor's desk by midnight.

So I went round the bases. And up (oh, just a few hellish times) at night with the crews. I flew. Saw. The whole works. Flak and tracer and vomit and kerosene and rear-gunners turned to meat. The photos on the desks, under the lamps and magnifiers, came alive and polychrome (so I could turn them into photos again), and I watched the light-show of Dresden burning, far below, in the dark.

Half my pictures, of course, they buried. You aren't supposed to see, let alone put on visual record, *those* things.

A photographer is neither there nor not there, neither in nor out of the thing. If you're in the thing it's terrible, but there aren't any questions, you do what you have to do and you don't even have time to look. But what I'd say is that someone has to look. Someone has to be in it and step back too. Someone has to be a witness.

SOPHIE

——

'Let's go back, Sophie, shall we? As far back as we can. Tell me about your earliest memories.'

'But that isn't a fair question.'

'How come?'

'Because how do you know, when you go back that far, that it's really memory? Not what you were told later, or what you've invented. Or just sheer fantasy.'

'Okay. Tell me your fantasy.'

'If you tell me yours.'

'You first.'

'Oh – you know – that everything was just fine, of course. That everything in the garden was lovely. Hasn't it got to be that way? So we can believe we come from Paradise? Then it gets fucked later. You're not going to tell me that the first thing people are going to remember, even if it *is* the first thing they remember, is the first Bad Time they ever had?

'You see, I had this wonderful Mummy and Daddy. Straight from a fairy tale. He was English, she was Greek. She was beautiful and he was handsome. And they'd met long ago, in Germany, and fallen in love, and got married all in a rush, and he brought her back with him to live in London.

51

'Shouldn't that be the most beautiful story there is? The story of how your mother met your father. The story of how you came to be. You know that line in the song? "Your Daddy's rich and your Momma's good-looking. So hush little baby . . ." Save that Harry wasn't rich. He was – but this is Harry's version, not mine – disinherited. Isn't that a great old word, Doctor K – "disinherited"? And Grandad, according to him, was just being kind because of Mum and me.

'Okay, so he used to go off now and then, I never knew why, for a week at a time maybe. But I always thought that was a necessary process. Like he was some faithful knight-errant. He'd always come back to Mum. They'd kiss. And one day we'd all settle down together at Hyfield. That was what Mum wanted. I know. She loved the place. And I think that for a while Harry even wanted it too. He took me up to where he worked once, in Fleet Street. I couldn't have been more than four – how's this for a first memory? There was this big room with men and telephones, and another down below with machines rolling and thumping. I guess I cried. He held me tight. And he said something like: Everything from all over the world comes here.

'Or how about this? We're all sitting, the four of us, out on the lawn at Hyfield. Mum's wearing a blue dress. She has big, dark, wide eyes. (Do I have big, dark, wide eyes?) She says things to me in Greek and I can understand them. *"Élado poulákimou, chrysoulamou."* "Come here, my little bird, my little golden one." She's talking to Grandad and Harry's sitting there, just listening. I can see that Mum and Grandad are fond of each other and that this somehow brings Harry and Grandad together. They're drinking something out of a big glass jug with bits of fruit floating in it. They all laugh and I laugh too.

'Holidays. That's what I remember. We went down to Cornwall – two, three years running. Last time with the Irvings. A hotel on a cliff. Steps down to a beach. (Jokes about the

Beeches on the beach!) I was supposed to have nearly drowned there once, but I don't remember. Just Harry rushing suddenly into the water, and shouting at Mum who was swimming, further out, and grabbing me and carrying me up the beach. He held me so tight. Then Mum and Uncle Frank and Auntie Stella came clustering round and he held me so tight, as if he didn't want to let me go, even when Mum wanted to take me, and I cried. But I don't remember nearly drowning.

'I remember. I remember when the world was just sun and sand and sea and salt air. I remember when the world didn't exist except where I was. I remember all of us playing games with a beach-ball, and thinking the world was like a coloured beach-ball, you could catch it in your arms. And Uncle Frank putting me on his shoulders to carry me. And I remember Harry taking photos of me. Just holiday snaps. My hair blowing. Giggling, licking ice-cream. He used to take that kind of photo too. It's hard to think of him taking photos like that.'

HARRY

——

When you put something on record, when you make a simu-lacrum of it, you have already partly decided you will lose it.

When I am not with Jenny, when she is away for only one night visiting her mother in Bristol, I play the game of trying to imagine exactly how she looks. I never can. When I see her, she is always so much better than the picture in my head. But I don't know if this is good or bad. If it's good that reality outshines the image, or if the fact that I can't imagine her means that I don't know her.

I used to say once, on those few occasions when I was persuaded to make public statements, that photography should be about what you cannot see. What you cannot see because it is far away and only the eye of the camera will take you there. Or what you cannot see because it happens so suddenly or so cruelly there is no time or even desire to see it, and only the camera can show you what it is like while it is still happening.

She wants me to take 'real photographs' again. We climb up the hill behind the cottage, the wind is riffling and polishing the grass, and she says, pointing at the downs and the clouds and the shafts of sunlight probing through them, 'You could start right here.' And I say, 'Why?' And she says (as if I don't have eyes), 'Because it's beautiful.' And I say, 'So, if it's beautiful, why photograph it? If you have the reality, who needs the picture?'

She looks at me, the breeze catching her hair, and I know what she's thinking. That I have never taken a photograph of her.

Joe writes to me about every six months. I haven't seen Sophie for ten years; I've never seen my grandsons, Tim and Paul. But twice a year or so Joe writes these cryptic, diligent reports. In his last letter he said Sophie had had some 'trouble'. But I was not to worry. It was okay. She was going to an analyst. I wonder: 'going to an analyst'? Problem solved or problem continuing? Or whether it's just some kind of announcement of status. Like saying: And now we have our own speedboat.

I'm not to worry. He wouldn't tell me if I should. His letters are imbued with confident good cheer.

I don't think he tells Sophie he writes to me. I don't reply and I don't think he expects me to. I haven't worked out his tenacious mixture of motives. He is sorry for me? He wants to sting my conscience? He hopes by this process of rationed, honourable communication to hold me at bay, so I will never suddenly intrude on whatever life they have made for themselves over there. Or that if some belated reunion should occur, he will be seen, like some fairy godfather, to have worked quietly, patiently for it to happen?

Is he a good man? I don't know. I used to call him 'the holiday merchant'.

And what – or who – did I want for Sophie anyway? That she should have gone to university in '66 and become a true, hip child of those high, heady times? And suffered the discomfort and the dilemma of being both the daughter of her father and the grand-daughter of her grandfather. I can see now why she never hurried back from that trip to Greece,

56

eager to join the liberated generation that was just turning Harry Beech into one of its minor idols.

She went to Greece to find her mother. To-find Anna. But she didn't find her mother. She found Joe. Joe and Argosy Tours. And she married him in '67.

That summer I'd got my sun-tan in the Sinai Desert, snapping young Israeli soldiers, whooping and singing, racing armoured cars over undefended sand, not believing war could be so easy. But I was there that September, in that same Surrey church, to give my daughter away. (Give her away?)

She linked her bride's arm in mine. I squeezed it. And it was strange how, in spite of ourselves, in spite of our first forced, let's-pretend smiles, the occasion conspired to make it seem that we had always been that close. As if it were our reunion.

A high street photographer, unctuous, fussy, bow-tied, took the pictures, never looking me once in the eye, and my heart went out to him.

I thought of how Anna and I were married, frugally if gladly, in that makeshift chapel in Nuremberg, and how later she regretted never having had the full, white, dressed-up English performance. The church porch, the bells, the tables laid on the lawn at Hyfield. She would have liked that, for Uncle Spiro's sake. Sent him the photos to gratify his old, Anglophile feelings.

In my morning suit and grey tie I must have looked dressed for the wrong part. Dad looked like the old soldier who might suddenly start to weep. Joe looked like the original lucky man.

And whatever Joe thought of me, whatever Sophie had told him about me, he must have blessed his luck that Sophie was the grand-daughter of Robert Beech. In '71 Dad put money into Argosy Tours. I know that. Just when Argosy Tours was starting to look like a shaky investment. A separate and discreet transaction, so you could never have said it was BMC money shoring up people's escapes to the sun. And not enough to stop the crash three years later. But enough to buy Joe time to make other arrangements and get out before things looked messy.

Not that there wasn't, suddenly, a far worse mess. A quite different mess. But even then some hidden part of him must have been counting his luck. He had fixed by then that job in New York. He had nobly declined, more than once, Irving's offer of a job at BMC. Unentangled. It was even luck that he wasn't there that morning at Hyfield. Though he kept repeating obstinately afterwards: I should have been there, I should have been there. As if there were some desperate magic he might have employed to prevent it all. Whereas his whole dazed demeanour was actually saying something else: I don't want to be here. I'm not really here, am I, Harry?

I see him coming out of that hospital ward where Sophie is lying groggy with shock and sedation, and his own look of shock hardens for an instant into one of absolute and infantile hate. As if *I* were to blame, I'd caused it all, I was the Jonah who'd put the ship smack on the rocks.

How much did she say?

And I see him the next night at the same hospital, when they let her go. My God, how I envied him that arm round her waist. She looked right through me, she looked at me as if she didn't know me. But he'd recovered by then. Had a role by then. There was that little glint of unextinguished luck in his eye. Sophie is okay. And the baby's okay. And if I can just hang on for however long this nightmare takes to fade, I really won't be here any more, we'll all be far away, in another continent, on the other side of the Atlantic.

Now he sits in a New York office, offering credulous Americans the charms of cosy old England. While I sit in a Wiltshire cottage which might be a picture from one of his brochures come to life.

Eight years ago I actually spoke to him. His voice came piping down the telephone from a London hotel. Till then his letters had been sent care of UPI, and I don't know how he got my number. He was over on business, by himself. Perhaps we could –? I made some excuse. I couldn't have borne his bright, lucky face. Wouldn't have known how to compose my own when he told me how the twins were growing. I said, Give them all my love, would you?

That was the summer Argosy Tours finally went under. And it occurred to me afterwards that, even though he'd left Argosy three years before, that might have been his 'business'. It was also the summer the Turks invaded Cyprus and the Junta fell in Greece. And if we'd met I might have asked him a question I'd always meant to ask him.

(No, Harry. You think everything's got to be connected? It just happened at that time. The whole tourist thing hit Greece at that time. There was competition. There was an oil crisis. Mind you, Cyprus was a risk . . .)

I might even have been there myself. In Cyprus. One more time. Taking shots for UPI of Turkish troops commandeering hotels and foreign-owned villas, and of that other contingent that hadn't been there in '57, in '64 – the baffled, stranded, indignant tourists.

But I had stopped all that. No news work, no photo work of any kind (the offers came, then petered out). I was making other arrangements. I was facing up to life in a picture-book cottage. Breathing country air. Meeting new neighbours. Like Doctor Warren. Yes, that's all, just some sleeping pills. Isn't it strange, Doctor, I can't sleep, here, where it's all so peaceful?

I might have travelled. I mean: just travelled. Been a tourist too. (Hang it, Harry, we all need a holiday some time.) Might have gone to Greece, like Sophie (but eight years later), to find Anna. But I don't believe in ghosts. I don't believe that Anna is up there on Olympus, watching Jenny and me descend a breezy hill in Wiltshire. No one knows about Anna.

I was trying to sleep, and have sweet dreams. I was trying to piece together my nerves and wondering how people ever contrive that impossible trick called Where I Live. I was lying awake haunted by the noise of owls and foxes. I would go for long, determined walks and watch the silver clouds gliding over green hills, rooks flapping over gnarled trees, and say to myself: I don't believe this. I would come back to the cottage, open the front gate, walk through the picture-book façade and crawl into the tent of myself.

SOPHIE

But there are certain things that you'll never remember, aren't there, Doctor K? All you know is that they must have happened. Like trying to remember the point at which you fell asleep. I don't remember when I first realized that Mum was never coming back. But maybe it wasn't a realization, just a knowledge that seeped into my mind. Like the knowledge that Harry was never going to be at home much any more, he was never really going to be my father again. He'd done some deal – that's how it seemed – struck some bargain with Grandad about being my father. He hadn't found Mum and brought her home, but he still kept going away – out of guilt maybe. So perhaps if I'd said to him, It's all right, Harry – it's all right, Dad – you don't have to be guilty about Mum, I know she's dead really, he might have come back to stay for good. But by this time I'd grown to like having Grandad as my father, and I'd grown to realize – and the feeling was mutual – that I was the most precious thing he had.

Like I was never really afraid of his arm. I mean, his artificial arm. It was something different, something special about Grandad. I wasn't afraid to touch it, to hold his cold, hard hand. And because I'd never known him without it, for a long time it never even occurred to me that once he must have had two real arms. He must have been waiting for the question to come, rehearsing the answer. Grandad, what happened to your arm? What he said was: Oh, I swapped it for a medal. Then he showed me the medal. It seemed such a drab little thing, a bit of dull metal and dull red ribbon, to swap for a whole arm. I didn't know then it was a Victoria Cross, or what you had to do to get a Victoria Cross.

This was up in the study, surrounded by Uncle Edward's, I mean, Great-uncle Edward's books. He got the medal out of a little hinged box from one of the drawers of his desk. Then he showed me a photograph and said, Guess who this is? And the strangest thing about the photograph wasn't that it was Grandad, taken years and years before, or that in it he had two arms – there it was, his real right arm, holding up a cigarette. The strangest thing was the face. The face was alive. Compared to the face of the Grandad I knew, that I was looking at right then, the face in the photograph was alive.

I don't remember him ever telling me what he did. I mean, what he did at his office in London. Or what they did at 'the factories'. Do you think he was always waiting to tell me that too? The right moment. Hoping perhaps he might never have to tell me, that I need never know. Just like me and the twins. All I knew was that every weekday he'd put on this smart suit and Ray would drive him up to town. Because in those days there wasn't a trace of BMC at Hyfield itself. It was only much later, after Joe and I got married and got our place in Richmond, that he started to turn it into a sort of company headquarters. That's what the papers called it: 'Family home of the Beeches and unofficial headquarters of BMC'.

Harry used to call it 'the arsenal'.

But even if I'd known – even when I did know – why should it have made any difference, why should I have given a damn? You judge by what you see, don't you? And you see what's closest first.

It must have seeped slowly into my mind too, so slowly you could almost ignore it, you could almost pretend you didn't really know it. I can't remember ever saying to myself, sitting on the terrace or under the apple trees in the orchard or looking out of the window as the rain fell on the lawn: Don't be fooled by all this, don't be taken in, remember what all this is made of.

But I remember, perfectly clearly, as if it were yesterday, that June morning when Grandad said, 'Come with me.' I remember the clean white shirt he was wearing with the dark green tie and the dog-tooth check trousers – they were not his 'office' clothes, even if this was, technically, an 'office' day. I remember the dew on the lawn and the sun just peering above the elms (it was not yet eight o'clock) and the air shivery yet gentle, as if Grandad had arranged, too, the promise of a perfect summer's day. I remember his slow yet jaunty, teasing step. I remember the spiders' webs glinting under the eaves of the stable, and every tuft of moss between the cobbles of the stable yard, and Ray standing there, waiting for us. And I remember the smell as we approached the stable door – a real stable door now, newly painted, not just the entrance to a store-shed. An unmistakable smell, a brown, warm, living smell.

Grandad opened, gently, the upper flap of the door and said, 'Now look inside.' But you didn't need to. Because there, nudging forward to poke its head out, so the sunlight caught its wet nostrils and its chocolate eyes and the tuft of mane falling between them, was a pony.

Ray came a little closer and Grandad stood very still. Perhaps they were afraid I might be afraid. But I put out my hand, and it seemed to want to be stroked. It cocked its head to one side and I felt its rough lip against my bare arm. Then Grandad said, 'Happy Birthday, my angel.' And Ray said, 'Happy Birthday, Miss Sophie.'

I was ten years old. Ten years old exactly. I don't know

where Harry was then, but he wasn't there for his daughter's birthday, and I didn't believe Grandad when he said the pony was from both of them, from Harry as well.

Ray, who must have been carefully briefed, slipped a halter over the pony's neck and gave the end to me. I led it round the yard, and Grandad said we had made good friends. I was all choked up with excitement. Then he said, if I could tear myself away, we would come back in a little while, but first he had something else to show me. We put the pony back in the stable and went back to the house. And there on the dining-room floor – Mrs Keane must have been briefed too – was a new saddle, bridle, girth, stirrups, cap, boots . . .

I remember the smell of the new leather, the sun on the blue and red carpet. And feeling Grandad's hand on my head as I knelt down to look at this hoard of gifts, and looking up and seeing him smile, and thinking, for some reason: He is as happy as I am, he is exactly as happy as I am.

On the table, laid for breakfast, was a huge vase of roses, and by my place was a little pile of envelopes. The top envelope was pale blue with strange stamps on it, and Grandad said I should open it first. Inside the envelope was a card and also a letter. It's funny, I don't remember what that letter said at all.

Then Mrs Keane brought in the breakfast, and Grandad said that after breakfast, which I couldn't eat fast enough, we would go and see how good I was at riding. Then he would take me somewhere nice for lunch. But I must be careful not to eat too much because at four o'clock, of course, there was my tea party, all my friends from school were coming and Uncle Frank and Auntie Stella and their little daughter Carol. If it was fine, which it looked like being, Mrs Keane and Ray would put tables outside, and, of course, everyone would want to see my pony. But in the meantime shouldn't we think up a name for him.

We called him Tony. Get it? Tony the pony.

You see, I was spoilt. I was a spoilt little brat. I was brought up like a princess in a palace and had everything I could ask for. Save, of course, a mother – and a father.

Palace? But you won't quibble over a Queen Anne house with oak panelling and a gravel drive and a lawn with two cedar trees, and a walled garden with a pond and a yew-tree walk and an orchard and paddock, and a stable and stable yard, no longer used as such when Grandad became their owner, but reconverted just before my tenth birthday to accommodate a pony and, three years later, a horse. Called Hadrian. That's palace enough when you're ten years old and when – with the addition of a housekeeper, a chauffeur-cum-valet and the part-time presence of two gardeners – only you and your grandfather have the run of it.

Hyfield House, built in 1709 by Nicholas Hyde, Gent. Let's face it, Doctor K, you can't *get* that sort of thing over here. The genuine, historical, English thing. You know, Joe and I used to joke that if Hyfield ever really became ours, we wouldn't have to look any further. It would just be the start. Some glossy advertising in the right places. One- or two-week rentals to rich and impressible Americans. The real, authentic, country-house experience.

Just a joke, of course. I said to Joe, You're not hiring out my Hyfield, my childhood. Over my dead body.

Over Grandad's dead body! Ha ha! But then, I guess they'd pay more, wouldn't they? If they knew it was the former residence of Robert Beech, v.c., hero and true British gentleman. Some gory history. A ghost. And this is the very spot where . . .

Just a joke. We'd never have thought then that that was actually what Joe would be doing one day. Castles and manor houses. Up-market vacations. Be a squire or a laird. Take a break from the twentieth century.

Yet if you want to know, that's how I used to think of

Hyfield once. I had this thing about the past. It used to be a good refuge, once, the past. I used to clop across the stable yard on Tony, and later on Hadrian, and make-believe it was the reign of Queen Anne. I used to imagine I was Mrs Hyde, wife of Nicholas Hyde. Mistress of the manor.

Maybe that's how I should begin. When I tell the boys. If I tell the boys. Let's go right back to the very start, shall we? Once upon a time, in the reign of good Queen Anne . . . Can you picture it? The world is safe and small – it only stretches to the next hill! The sky is blue – of course it's blue! But this is pure, clear eighteenth-century blue, and the white clouds that float across it aren't just clouds, they are time passing very slowly, the way time once used to pass. The apples are ripening in the orchard, the stooks are standing in the field. In the yew-walk, arm in arm, Mr and Mrs Hyde (but let's call them Beech) are strolling, she in her hooped dress and bonnet, he in his cocked hat and breeches. And all is as it should be . . .

I can't think what it's like now. With Frank there. They'll have patched up the frontage and the porch. All weathered in – no trace perhaps.

The last time I saw it as it *was*, the last time I saw that old world, my past, was that Sunday, that very last Sunday. And I had actually come to say I didn't want it. Chose a good time, didn't I? I was quite sure – now the future was fixed: Joe, me, New York – that I didn't want it. But by then it was almost understood between Grandad and me, almost expected, part of our little scheme of renunciation; and the real reason I was there that morning was to tell him something else about my future: that I was pregnant.

I wanted him to be the first to know. Got that? After Joe, I mean. Though I happened to know full well that Harry was, for once, in London right then, and it would – it should – have been the simplest thing to pick up the phone and say, Hi Dad, it's me. Guess what?

Shit! The whole world got to know! In less than forty-eight hours the whole world could read – it made such good copy – that Sophie Beech was pregnant. And had only just –

And, yes, I thought it often afterwards: What had been the point? What had been the goddam point of telling him about the baby he was never going to see? Which turned out anyway to be two not one. But now I think: No, it's the one thing I'm glad of. That at least he knew.

I said: 'I'm going to make you a great-grandfather.'

It would have to have been a perfect spring morning. Warm enough to sit outside and everything suddenly in leaf. As if the whole place were saying: Are you sure? Don't you want to think twice? In no time he had a bottle of champagne and two glasses on that little table out on the terrace. And I guess we were halfway through it before that other subject came up. I said, 'Perhaps now's the time –' And he said, 'I know.' But I wanted to say it. I said, 'It's all right. I don't want it. You know that. We know that. None of it.' And he said, 'Thank God.' And let out a great rough chuckle of relief which sent the pigeons flapping off the orchard wall. 'So Frank gets the lot. Let him have it. All of it. Let the company have it.' He took a gulp of champagne. Then he said, 'Now I've got something to tell you, Sophie. I'm getting out. Not just saying it this time. I'm actually at long last, officially, finally going to retire. Shall we drink to that too?'

Okay, Doctor K – so we should believe in fate? *That* kind of fate? And what was the truth? That he was seventy-three years old and BMC had been his life anyway? Or that it was a fifty-years-and-more pretence and he was just about to be a real man again?

I think of that photo. His face in that photo.

He poured the last of the champagne. Using his metal arm. A trick he liked. Look at my latest toy. I make a good robot, don't I?

67

'Have you told Harry?'

'What do you think?'

He smiled. This was how it was between us when we talked about Harry.

'Well, you'll have a chance to tell him tonight. He'll be here. You know – just passing through. Between planes. Why don't you stay here tonight?'

'I have to get back.'

'What's Joe doing?'

'He's with the American people.'

'So – all the more reason. Give him a call. Look, if you like, I'll pretend, for Harry's sake, that you haven't told me either.'

Then he said: 'I'll miss you in the States.'

But he wouldn't, would he?

I stayed. I told Harry. I didn't say: 'I'm going to make you a grandfather.' I just said, 'I'm pregnant.' And do you know what his very first reaction was to those words – the very first, brief look in his eyes? I'd swear it was alarm, I'd swear it was something almost like fright. He was passing through, all right. His bags and cameras with him. Catching a plane the next morning. And do you know where he was going? Belfast. Jesus Christ! Belfast!

Grandad went through his little act. Fetched a fresh bottle of champagne – as if we hadn't been drinking the stuff all afternoon. But I guess he was happy then, too. I guess he was as happy as he was ever likely to be.

And there we were. All three Beeches, in the family house. Grandfather, father and daughter. Even two little unborn semi-Beeches, pretending to be one. That was the night of 23rd April, 1972. Springtime in England – St George's day! And under the back seat of the Daimler there was a bomb, and nobody knew.

HARRY

——

But he really died three times. He really had three turns with death. The second was in '45, nearly thirty years after the first, and maybe it was the worst – and the best – of the three. The worst, because he knew, or thought he knew, what was happening: he was lying there on his back with death hovering over him and somewhere in the space he could see, too, whatever there had been of his life. And the best, because, after a certain point at least, he knew he wasn't really going to die. It was the *idea* that was special. Since that first time, I think, he never cared two hoots about the fact. But he had time, now, to think of the idea. And it was the idea that gave him power. It was a trump card which he played for all it was worth.

Compassionate leave! Isn't that the most grotesque of notions? You are up in the night sky, watching cities burn, planes and men get ripped, then your father has a heart attack and you get leave for compassion. The telegram reached me at two in the afternoon and the leave followed almost immediately. All that evening on the train down to London I was working hard at the compassion.

And he must have been working on the big death-bed scene. He was only forty-six, which was perhaps sure enough guarantee that he would pull through. But I had never thought of him as anything other than an old man, an old man who'd become an old man some time around the time of my birth. So it never occurred to me to treat the occasion as an extreme sort of hoax.

He lay propped against the pillows, in a private room, surrounded by the apparatus that they surrounded such patients with then. He was asleep. Or at least, his eyes were closed and his chest was heaving. I remember that his metal arm lay, detached, beside him on the bedside table. Like the sword of a dying knight. Either he or the hospital had decided that he should die without his armour. But it lay there, pathetically, beside him. And I remember feeling a stab of pity for that bereft arm that I did not feel for my father.

I said, 'Dad?' And he opened his eyes and recognized me, and said, 'It's you.' We looked at each other. Then he said, 'I haven't much time.' And when I heard those absurd words, like something out of a cheap play, I knew he wasn't really going to die.

He didn't want compassion and he didn't want forgiveness. What he wanted was sworn promises. He wanted me to swear that I would take over at BMC. That when he was gone and the Air Force released me, I would fill his place. I said, as quietly as I could, that we had been through all this before. Besides, I knew now what I did want to do – the last few weeks had confirmed it: I wanted to be a photographer. I didn't say witness, observer, neutral party, floating pair of eyes. He almost screamed at me: Photographer! And then he switched, as I knew he would, on to the loyalty and ingratitude tack. How it had been a family firm, a Beech firm, for seventy years etc., how he'd put his all into it etc. etc., and why did I think he was lying there stricken by a heart attack, if it wasn't from overwork, from sheer damn hard work, six relentless years of wartime production. Breaking all records.

70

I watched his lips working, his jaw held up, his Adam's apple moving up and down, knowing he knew that I knew that to cross him, to provoke him, under these circumstances, was effectively forbidden. I kept my voice as low as possible and said that whatever else there might be between us, there was a matter now of principle. I had seen a little of what bombs did, I didn't think I wanted to spend my life making them. And he laughed at that, laughed out loud at that, and said how did I imagine we had won the war except by dropping bombs? Or did I think we shouldn't have won it! And he called that kind of thinking 'gutless'. Gutless.

The word seemed to leave him without breath. He just lay there, exhausted and helpless, only his eyes burning ferociously. Then he said those extraordinary words, so extraordinary that if they hadn't been spoken so softly, so deliberately, I would have laughed out loud too. He said, 'I love my country.' And again: 'I love my country.'

I don't know if he really did believe at that moment that his time was up. Or whether it was all part of the tableau he was staging. The old campaigner's fighting farewell. But just for an instant I thought his eyes were no longer fierce. They were saying: Harry, get me out of this, get me out of this *person*. As if his lips had been trying to utter something else, but what came out, with such perverse, measured sincerity, was 'I love my country'.

I edged closer. I felt I should take his hand. I said quietly, 'It's all right.' And as soon as he heard this, the fierceness came back, quick as lightning. 'So do you promise?' he said. 'Do you promise?'

I said, 'Don't force me, Dad. Don't blackmail me.'

He didn't die, of course. The old bastard lived on, with occasional maintenance work on his heart, till he was seventy-three. And even then –

He said, 'If you walk out of this room it'll be the last time

71

you see me. And if you walk out of this room without giving me your promise, you won't get a thing. Not a damn thing. Do you hear? How much do you think a photographer makes? Eh? Eh?'

And I thought: He can't actually change it. He can't come out of it, cast it aside. Not even now. Not even when – He's got to go through with it, sound off like some demented Victorian Papa. He's played the part so long he doesn't know any more if it's him or not. I knew I was going to walk out of that room.

My God! My God, Jenny! My God, Sophie! How terrible to die, how terrible to be dying and not to know, at the end of it all, what is true or false.

SOPHIE

—

A toy gun in a Brooklyn yard. A toy gun in the land of guns. They won't ever forget that day, will they, Doctor K? One of them brings home a toy gun – and it's only a *borrowed* toy gun – and they're playing shoot-outs in the backyard, and their mother who's watching through the kitchen window suddenly flips, she goes right off her head.

Two things I've never allowed in the house. Toy guns (six-shooters, rifles, machine-guns or any form of toy weaponry). And cameras.

Joe said we shouldn't have a thing about it. Maybe having a thing about it was worse. Because it was only natural for kids to play fight-games, and maybe it was actually better, getting it all out in a game, in harmless fun. And in any case, what was to stop them simply putting two fingers together and pointing – 'using their imagination' he called it! – and making those Krrrsh! Kpow! noises? And I said, well that was all very well and, yes, if every man who'd ever played with a toy gun actually progressed to the real thing, then the world would be a far sight bloodier than it is. But it didn't mean every kid should have one. And if people say, well a toy is a toy, pretend is pretend and real is real, then what about those kids you see on the news with little old hard faces, only eleven or twelve but they're dressed up in combat gear and they're toting real machine-guns around the way other kids tote baseball bats. And what about this story – have you heard it? – it's a true story. A man goes into a store and points a gun at the store-keeper and the store-keeper hands over all the cash he has. Then, before he makes off, the man squirts water from the gun into the store-keeper's face. Ha ha! he says, Not real, you see! But the store-keeper dies from a real enough heart attack.

Cameras, though. That's more complicated, isn't it? When every true American child, brought up within a certain income bracket, is directing their first home movie at least by the age of fourteen. Watch them in front of the TV. Lifting the cookies to their mouths without even moving their eyes. You got some-thing to tell us, Mom? To explain? What, now? While we're watching –

Dear Doctor K, you say such wise, such clever things. I wish I could say such things. Like: 'Life is a tug of war between memory and forgetting.' Like: 'What you are afraid of, Sophie, is to leave the cocoon of surrogate amnesia provided by your children's ignorance.' Wow! And fuck you too. You used to put your cool, papery palm on my hot forehead, as if you could draw out the trouble with just a lift of your hand . . .

To remember – that can be bad, Sophie. And to forget – that can be bad too. Isn't that the problem? Either way, you're in a mess. But the answer to the problem is to learn how to tell. It's telling that reconciles memory and forgetting. Sophie, let us try a little experiment. Let us suppose that I am that part of you which wants to forget: yet which, deep down, would really like to hear what another part of you is longing to tell. Or – one step further – let us suppose that I am your two twin boys, Tim and Paul, your two dear boys who are waiting to hear the story that you know one day you must tell them. You have been putting it off and putting it off, and so long as they ask no

74

questions, so long as they remain in happy ignorance, it is as though you too can believe that certain things never happened.

Dear Doctor Klein, I would happily lie back on that couch of yours, in that cocoon of yours above 59th Street, and let you tell me a story. Hush little baby. A bedtime story . . .

Once upon a time in the reign . . .

My darling Tim and Paul. I want to thank you for nine years of Safety. That's what I gave myself – eight, nine, maybe ten years. When you grow up, my darlings, you'll find out that at the beginning there were the years without any memory at all. And then even when memory began, there were the years without wanting or caring specially to know. Your gift to your mother. She needed a rest from memory.

I knew one day my time would be up. I thought one day you must just say: Tell us about England, tell us about where we come from. (Like: Tell us about the facts of life.) Or one day you'd find somewhere a copy of *Aftermaths* or *Photos of a Decade* (you won't find a copy in the house). And you'd say: Did Harry really take these pictures? Hey, tell us about Harry. (Harry is your grandfather, my angels.) Faces frightened? Agog? Or just mildly curious? Pictures like that are just two-a-penny now, aren't they?

I never thought my time would come up like it did. A toy gun.

And a letter.

Dear boys. I don't allow cameras in the house, but your mother still takes her mental photographs, still puts on mental film her *aides-mémoire* of your ignorant, growing years. As now, through the kitchen window, where in the fading Brooklyn evening you are playing with your father (no gun this time) in the yard. A rough and ready game of soccer (in deference to Joe who still follows the fortunes of Tottenham Hotspur). Tim and Paul. Dark shocks of hair, dark eyes. Like your mother's, and her mother's. It was a kind of recompense perhaps, nature's

75

double peace-offering for the agonies of that spring and summer: twins. Twins! And it was only because you were twins that I didn't, in the end, call either of you what I would certainly have called you if you'd only been one: Robert.

Joe, gallantly defending the apple-tree goal-mouth. Fair hair, touched with grey. Paler skinned than his sons and reddening more quickly. Handsome about the eyes still, and still sometimes, as now when he's locked in this boys' game, boyish and mobile around the mouth. It used to please me once, to excite me, that combination. It was so good to meet a man who simply didn't have the knack of setting his mouth and jaw in that grave, grim, piously masculine way. Who could actually say and mean it, with never an inch of tongue in his cheek: This is a good time to be born in, this is the age of Fun! As if he would always be young. As if despite all his efforts to be the slick, shrewd man-of-the-world, innocence would perversely win and he would never lose the conviction that he had been set down in some vast playground.

Pouring out the wine and piling his plate high – *barbounia*! *garithes*! *kalamarákia*! – in that taverna by the waterfront under the stars in Poros. Touching me up under the table. Isn't life grand, isn't life just a peach? *Omorfí i zoí*!

He couldn't believe his luck – dizzy with luck upon luck – when I said, Yes. Yes.

And now it disturbs me (it shames me) when I see it. That smile like a boy's.

He lets in a header from Paul. Mops his brow. Laughs.

A perfect snapshot. Framed in the kitchen window. The laughing father, the laughing sons.

An image, my dear Sophie, is something without knowledge or memory. Do we see the truth or tell it?

And would that image through the window still be the same if those two happy boys knew what their mother knows (and will tell them), looking at them through the glass? And would it be the same image if the father, who knows what the mother knows, didn't have the knack – I don't know what it really is, a sort of generosity or a sort of stupidity – of ignoring what he knows and endorsing only the image?

'Things Not to Miss in Beautiful Britain.'

You can shoot with both. You can load and aim with both. With both you can find your target and the rest of the world goes black.

First Tony the pony. Then Hadrian the horse. I used to ride round the paddock, then along the bridleway, over the heath. Can you imagine that? A real English heath. Crisp winter sunlight. Frost melting on the gorse and bracken. I haven't ridden for years, but I love horses. Sometimes I think I should have been born in the age of horses. That's what Grandad said, when I asked him more about the medal: It was worse for the horses. I didn't understand. But I had this picture of a whole lost age of horses.

Over the heath, down the dip, along by the wood. Don't let anyone kid you, Doctor K, that there's nothing sexual about little girls and horses. I first menstruated on a horse. So – she told me after Grandad's seventieth: I was drunk and I said, 'Snap!' – did Carol Irving.

I was Mrs Hyde. Grandad was Nicholas Hyde. Then one summer a stranger from the future came to visit. Harry. He was sun-tanned but he didn't look as if he'd been on holiday. He watched me ride, but never came near – do you know something? I think he was *scared* of horses – and asked me about school, and sat talking with Grandad. He didn't have his camera, but he had this portfolio, full of photos, with the rest of his things up in the bedroom. I wasn't supposed to look. But I wanted to know about my father. And now I did.

Another image for you. A pair of images. Overlaid upon each other. The sun flickering through the cedar tree and entering that bedroom at Hyfield. Harry's things, like the belongings of some lodger. The man lying on the hot white sidewalk. They called it 'that famous shot'. In *Aftermaths* all it says is 'Oran, 1960'. The sound of Grandad's and Harry's voices from below. Face up, his arms outspread and ankles crossed, and from the back of his head that long, long dark stream, stretching, stretching as if it will never end, down the street. I didn't know which was worse, that the world contained such things or that my father had taken that picture.

HARRY

Miracles shouldn't happen. Picture-books aren't real. The fairy-tales all got discredited long ago, didn't they? There shouldn't be thatched cottages still, tucked away among green hills. You shouldn't be able to advertise in the local papers for an assistant and fall in love with the very first candidate who comes along. I should have gone on, in fairness, to consider Applicant Two and Applicant Three, since all I wanted (honestly Michael, truly Peter) was a competent part-time assistant. But I found out that, after all, I was still human.

Vacancy filled.

As if I should have resorted to the lonely hearts columns, and discovered, at the first attempt, lo and behold, my heart was cured of its loneliness . . .

'Supposing you had been Number Three?'

'You mean you wouldn't have chosen me?'

'No, I mean supposing you had been Number Three and I had chosen Number Two.'

'Then you would never have known me.'

'I can't imagine never having known you.'

Three days a week. Paperwork. Film processing. Sometimes at the cottage by herself, while I was seeing clients or in

79

the air. I used to think: She's there, she's there right now.

Two, three weeks of playing it straight. Jenny, could you – ? Jenny, I'd like you to – This is how – Thank you, Jenny. Is it an infallible sign of love that it makes you feel again, even at sixty-three, like a clueless adolescent? A week of (not so subtle) inquiry. Her parents were divorced. She had a flat in Swindon where the family home had been and where she'd gone to art school. Boyfriends? No contenders at present. ('Why should that be surprising?') Another week of mutual suspicion that perhaps we knew each other's game: she was an independent girl with a thing about older (much older) men, especially solitary men with shadowy pasts, especially burnt-out, rough-edged photo-journalists. I was the sort of man who at a certain age hired help-mates for ulterior purposes. But was damn slow about it.

I took her one evening to the White Lion for dinner, because she had worked late. (Had I contrived – had she? – that it would be necessary to work late?) The landlord, in the saloon, poker-faced as he handed us the menus. And who should be sitting at a nearby table but Doctor and Mrs Warren (both nodding politely and both plainly inquisitive), tucking into roast duck?

She said, 'I hope I'm not damaging your reputation.'

I said I didn't know I had one to protect.

She raised an eyebrow. More curious than sly.

'But then the village gossip is hardly going to bother *you*.'

She looked at me as if this was an opening to tell her the whole story of my life.

A photographer's groupie? Such creatures existed, certainly, back in the news-chasing days. Though I never – Women, certainly. (Yes, Michael, if you want to know . . .) Women in strange rooms and strange beds, and non-beds, in I've forgotten how many strange places. Women with no names. Waking up in sticky dawns and trying to focus on where the room is and who the woman is. Shaking her awake, getting up and stubbing your toe on a half-drained bottle which skitters across the floor. You don't expect to do this thing, to do this stuff, do you, and then go calmly to bed at night with a mug of cocoa and a good read? Bodily needs. For the nerves. But nothing more. Here's your money, so you can go now, so I can forget you. Yes, good boom-boom, number-one long-time. Thank you. I'm bound up with this thing, hooked on it now, it's rubbed off on me so much there's nothing much left of *me* any more. Just the eyes. I'm not afraid out here, you see. I get afraid in Surrey lanes. I was brought up in the finest English traditions. Yes, I had a wife once. Take the money, please . . .

The White Lion Inn. Oak beams and horse brasses. Jenny pressing a glass of red wine to her cheek.

But she would have been too young. Only twelve or thirteen when I packed it in. Might never even have looked at a copy of *Aftermaths* or *Decade*, both of which, I suspect, are now acquiring rarity value.

Her eyes go sharp and shrewd, soft and artless by turns. These days I don't know if twenty-three is still young. Or if the young have any innocence any more.

A week of thinking: So don't be a fool, don't be a damn fool. And then a week of quiet agony (surely mutual? surely mutually detectable?) because it seemed that I might – that we might – let something real slip away simply out of the fear that it might not be real. Then a week when the argument turned inside out and I said to myself: Don't be a fool, don't be a fool – how would you feel if she didn't even come three days a week, to be under your roof? And the answer shot back: Empty, bereft.

In the pub car park, when I pulled her towards me, she said, 'My God, I thought you'd never – '

I said (but this was later, in the dead of night: her car still parked on the road outside, the keys to her flat somewhere amongst the clothes on the floor): 'How long has this been going on?'

'About six weeks.'

'Me too.'

'But who's counting?'

(An owl's hoot in the distance. The whole world of her small body letting me in, letting me come in. Strange bits of my life spilling, now, out of my lips.)

'This is crazy. I'm forty years older than you.'

'Who's counting?'

Now look at Harry Beech. Former rover of the world, former witness to its traumas and terrors. He steps from the back door of a country cottage, dressed only in a dressing-gown and old slippers, to tip bits of bread and bacon rind on to the bird-table in the garden. He sniffs moist Sunday morning air. Inspects spring bulbs. As he stands at the bird-table he hears a knocking at a window, and turns and looks up at the bedroom. He sees a face, a sleepy, smiling, brown-haired, blue-eyed face. Framed in the window, it is like a living portrait. He stands, holding a bread-board, amazed by a single face. All the faces, all the faces, all the shouting, screaming, frightened, weeping, dying, dead faces. Nothing is more exquisite than a single human face. The face comes close to the window. Below the face are bare shoulders, bare breasts. The face blows him a kiss.

Now look at Harry Beech, sitting at his kitchen table (while outside the birds of Wiltshire contend at the bird-table). He is writing a letter. Struggling with the words. (The first of its kind for ten years.)

Dear Sophie. How can I tell you? How can I say this? Your father, who you haven't seen for ten years and who is sixty-four years old, is going to get married. And she is almost half your age. And a third of his. And though we haven't told anyone yet, and we haven't fixed a day, I was wondering, we were wondering – I was hoping – If, after all this time –? If –?

SOPHIE

—

I can tell you exactly when Harry gave up photography. Just as exactly as I can tell you when it was I last saw him. They were almost one and the same.

But why did he have to be there at all? Why when he was never around for the rest of the time did he have to show up for the grand occasions? Weddings. And funerals. Like when he led me to the altar to marry Joe. I didn't want him there, didn't want him throwing his shadow on it all. But I was surprised how well he carried it off. How good he looked. And just for a moment, as we entered the church and the organ started and, right on cue, he patted my hand that was hooked on to his arm, I thought – I couldn't help myself – he is doing this for me, he is making the picture right for me. I am this white, nervous, beaming bride leaning on the arm of her father. And everything is as it should be.

Shit! It was the same church. The same damned church. And we had to do the same thing – the father-and-daughter, the next-of-kin thing. I had to take his arm and we had to walk through the lych-gate, between the yew trees and holly bushes, up the path to the grave.

There were so many cars parked in the sunshine in the lane

by the church. So many black, chauffeur-driven cars. Except, of course, one. Ray would get driven, in a hearse all of his own, to Epsom crematorium.

Three, four police cars. And further down the lane, at a discreet distance, the press and TV contingent. They were supposed not to move in till the service was over. But it didn't stop them testing their equipment as the cortège glided past. Positioned like snipers, behind trees, hedges, on the roofs of their cars.

I thought I would never get through that day. I thought I would not be able to hold my head on my shoulders, to put one foot in front of the other. But as we ran that first little gauntlet I looked at Harry on the seat beside me, and I knew I would make it. His head was turned away from the window. Fuck you, Harry. Don't even you have the power to stop them? Your colleagues, your goddam accomplices! He was staring at the floor of the car. I knew from then on his helplessness would buoy me up. I knew I would make it because I could say to those eager pressmen at any time: Hey, you want a good story? I mean, another story, a spicy sub-story. It hasn't happened yet, but it's going to be called 'What Became of Harry Beech?'. You want the inside facts? You want to know how Harry Beech was the true journalist, the real professional, right up to the very end? Want to know what I know?

We had to walk through the lych-gate, Joe with Frank and Stella Irving behind us, following the coffin with its froth of flowers. So many wreaths, so many tributes. So many black cars glinting in the sun. And if half the language that was being used had actually taken solid shape, there'd have been muffled drums and plumes and rifle volleys.

How does it happen? How do our little lives get turned into these big shows? Even when all that's left of us is little pieces. How do they get made into public property?

We had to walk back again, afterwards, down the same path,

knowing that this time they were waiting in full ambush, clustered round the gate. Primed and loaded.

I was clutching his arm. But, you see, nobody could tell it was really the other way round. He was clinging on to me, and under the pressure my flesh was hardening, giving nothing. I was thinking: This is simple. This isn't real, I am simply not here. I am still in a white daze, I am still in the white, numb, noiseless daze that follows the blast of a bomb. When it clears, I'll be on the terrace again, with Grandad pouring champagne and saying he's getting out. I'm not here. I'm just watching this. But Harry's here. No longer just watching. He thinks he'll never get out of this churchyard.

Come on, Harry. Why so reluctant? Remember my wedding day. These are your pals here. No? You can't do it?

Very well, very well. I'll do it. If it helps. I'll go soft, I'll pretend I'm really leaning on you. I'll pretend to be faint with grief (as if I should be faint with grief!). I'll do it for you, and Frank and BMC and the whole, gawping British public. Since I can't do anything for Grandad right now.

It's amazing, isn't it, how you never know your own strength?

I leant. I let my legs go a little weak. The papers said: 'almost stumbled'. At the same time I lifted my hand to my face, because suddenly, like some fit of induced vomiting, I found I could cry. Simple.

We were almost at the gate when he said, so softly, under his breath (to me? to them?), 'No, please.' And as if that were a signal, they all fired away. Zap! Zap! Zap!

You should see the pictures, Doctor K. Look them up in back numbers. They're great pictures. He with his arm round me and me with my leg bent and my hand to my face. You wouldn't believe from those pictures that he was really clinging to me, or that something had finally snapped between us, and something had snapped inside him.

85

Snap shots! Ha ha!

And you wouldn't believe that that wasn't my grief – 'The Grand-daughter's Grief'. No, my grief wasn't on show. I was just crying for the cameras.

That was the moment, the precise moment. The end of Harry Beech, photographer.

But it wasn't the end of that long, dazed day. Or of our inane double act. We still had to stand staunchly together (the last of the Beeches!) at Hyfield, while the guests arrived with their rehearsed words and purified faces.

At Hyfield. Where else? Where the débris had only just been cleared and the damage hastily covered or repaired. Fresh gravel on the drive. And where the objection that it was all in the most dubious taste was countered by the very boldness of the gesture. Defiance in the ruins. 'Business as usual'. Echoes of former, testing times. As if the pocks in the walls and the scorch-marks on the lawn were only there to embellish the theme that had already been squeezed dry by the newpaper pieces and the TV clips. The old warrior. The one-armed hero. The true Brit.

Frank said, Leave it all to me. To us. To BMC. And I didn't have the voice to resist. I didn't even whisper the word 'private'. As new – as acting – Chairman: his duty. Robert had *been* the Company, hadn't he? I let him gently insist that public outrage, as well as corporate solidarity, could hardly be ignored. So, yes, there would be 'a few media people' present. And police too. Some in plain clothes. Some of them (as if this would comfort me) armed. I let him say, on my behalf, into microphones, before flash-lights: 'Mr Beech's grand-daughter is too distressed to answer questions.' (Funny, so was Harry Beech.) 'However, we at BMC most strongly . . .' I even let him feed them that tear-jerking bonus: my pregnancy. 'Her last words to her grandfather.'

That was the last time I thought of him as 'Uncle Frank'.

He was there, of course, circulating and officiating while Harry and I stood like dummies. You could see the exhaustion behind the attentiveness in his face. You should have been able to see fear too. Just a flicker, a shadow of fear. But it didn't show. As if he were high on some rare potion of invincibility. As if, because they'd got Grandad, they could never get him, and this whole day were some kind of lavish propitiation of the gods for his future.

Why not? It was a PR coup. BMC could do no wrong now, could it? And in any case, he had his prize. He must have known by then, without knowing what I knew, that Hyfield was his. On the Company. That even if Joe and I were to make a drastic change of plan, we would not want to live *here*. In this house where –

I didn't let him know I wasn't really there. I didn't tell him I hadn't come out of the white daze. Death isn't black, is it? It's white. It's the whitest, hottest, coldest, blindingest flash there is. I let him treat me as if he were still Uncle Frank, and I was little Sophie Beech who once used to perch on his shoulders. I let him take my arm and let his invincibility support me, just like Harry's helplessness. Let him cut in like some ballroom interloper and steer me round the Board members and the company veterans called out of retirement for the day and the young high-fliers. This is Sophie. Our prize asset.

I carried it off like an actress. Such dignity! Such courage! Such – in the circumstances – self-possession! The English are so wonderful, aren't they, Doctor K, at Events?

I don't know what happened to Harry. He just disappeared, melted away. But that was always his trick, wasn't it? The vanishing act. Grandad and I used to call him The Invisible Man. Perhaps he was wandering among the crowd, trying to be anonymous, trying to be just another one of them. Which wouldn't stop their eyes picking him out with a sort of wary fascination.

That's him. That's Harry Beech. He doesn't put bombs in cars. He just —

We came face to face in the drawing-room as the whole thing was winding up. People were leaving, moving to their cars, and Frank was saying, 'Go now, Sophie. You're exhausted. You've been marvellous.' (Never performed better.) 'You don't have to stay to the very end.' (So what end was that?) And Joe saying, as if he were actually standing there waving like some magic wand, in case I'd forgotten, two tickets to New York, two tickets to the Promised Land: 'Let's go, let's go.' Let's slip away, just you and I, from the party.

It's easy, it's simple: you just go away. You just make sure you're not at the scene. You just don't be there.

He looked stranded. So what's the matter, Harry, no home to go to? He held his arms outwards, like a pair of useless wings. I know what he wanted. He wanted to embrace me. So it would look right, there in front of everyone. Life is an act, isn't it? Life is a real act. For a moment, a deliberate moment, I let him flap his arms like that. And there was Harry Beech, so in his element wherever the action was, so always pressed up against the window of the news trying to get in, floundering, sinking, amongst the tea cups and sherry glasses in an English drawing-room. I said to myself: You're never going to see, you're never coming near your grandchild. Then I put out my hand. I saw the look in his eyes. He took it, pressed it. And I said, 'Goodbye. Harry.'

Father, Dad, Daddy.

HARRY

A hero's death. A martyr's death.

A hero chooses. A martyr chooses.

As if he had known. As if he had stepped out that morning and got into the Daimler with the express purpose of risking his life against the forces of terrorism. But didn't he do that every day? As a manufacturer and supplier of arms – to, amongst others, our lads in Ulster – wasn't he always putting himself in the exposed and dangerous front line? And let's have no shilly-shallying and no moral niceties. We need arms for our defence. We need arms to maintain law and peace.

Cut to 1941. A rare, brief clip of Robert Beech in a factory yard with Mr Winston Churchill (grey bowler, cigar primed). Factory girls, with head scarves, in the background, jostling and grinning – one waves a tiny Union Jack. Mr Churchill congratulates 'Bob' Beech on his production achievement. (A photo of the same scene, with the Churchill signature, framed, above his office desk in London.)

Cut to R.B. with Max Beaverbrook and Royal Ordnance directors outside sandbagged offices of the Ministry of Supply.

Cut, by way of photo-library material, to 1875. Beech Munitions Company founded. First factory near Woking,

Surrey. Early work in the development of the steel-cased shell and the use of cordite propellant and lyddite filling. Also in small-arms engineering. Beech armaments used in the Sudan and South Africa. Cut – cut (representative material: howitzers at Omdurman; Mafeking celebrations). Cut to group photo of Sandhurst cadets, circa 1916: Bob Beech amongst – second row left, blurred. Cut to all-purpose Western Front footage. 'In 1918 . . .'

There was the potent and self-damning irony of the I.R.A. choosing for their target an arms manufacturer. Since terrorists themselves, by definition, required arms, which had to be made by someone. An irony duly exploited but not over-stressed. Since it led, in one direction, to the spectre of the arms-maker as the patron of terrorism, a mercenary among mercenaries – hardly appropriate to a company which was by now virtually an agency of the Ministry of Defence. Which begged in turn the question of what other fields BMC was now operating in, and what exactly was its area of development. The impression was given that it was still churning out good old unobjectionable bullets for latter-day Tommy Atkinses. But – nothing ill of the dead.

And in answer to those coolly liberal elements who might have said (all things being equal, and without wishing to condone the I.R.A.), Why the fuss? If you deal in that trade, if you live by the sword – Ah yes, but he *did* live by the sword and he was prepared to die. He was, as we all know, a hero already. A Victoria Cross and a tin arm. A life member of the valour club. And who had a better right to make and trade in arms (no obvious puns please) than a decorated ex-soldier who had sacrificed a limb in his country's service?

A hero. He sat on ten pounds of gelignite.

And should you be getting too warlike a picture, consider the campaigner of peace.

Cut to period photos of: the new ('Robert Beech') Wing

(Amputees' Rehabilitation Centre) of the King George Hospital at Guildford, Surrey, opened 1925; the façade of the Institute for Artificial Limb Research at Chiswick, west London, established 1929. His involvement in medical research was not widely known. Particularly in the field of prosthesis and surgical reconstruction, where his own personal trauma (he himself was an enthusiastic guinea-pig) was naturally a prime motive. But the objects of Beech benevolence, to mention only the medical ones, were many and diverse, ranging from obstetrics to heart research (he suffered a near-fatal heart attack in 1945; was fitted with a pacemaker in 1968), and from plastic surgery to the funding of a company – virtually a Beech subsidiary – which specialized in the development of electrically powered wheelchairs and other invalid aids. Charity begins at home, and travels in strange ways, and it would be unfair to point out that numerous beneficiaries of Beech patronage, from hospital patients to schoolchildren, might have been surprised to learn what was the original source of their succour.

Cut to village children on the lawn at Hyfield, mid 1930s (local press material). Cut to local worthies with R.B. on same lawn, same period. Cut to general view of the house and grounds – 'his home for nearly fifty years'. Intersperse with film of the bomb-damaged façade, April 1972. Cut to shot of R.B. as parliamentary candidate, 1935. Voice-over quoting from election speech. Brief sequence illustrating impercipience of Baldwin and Chamberlain governments. A gentleman, a true Englishman of the old school, but not afraid to speak his mind or challenge the mood of the time, and no enemy of the modern. Cut to film (last known footage, by proficient amateur) of after-dinner speech, November 1969. He jokes about his pacemaker: 'Soon I will be all spare parts.' He speaks of the 'courage' (he uses that word) of science in penetrating the 'strongholds of romance'. The Apollo landings, the cardiac transplant. The moon. The heart.

Bluff old charmer. A still spry public man at over seventy. An enthusiast for the new, but an avowed critic of what he called Britain's post-war 'relaxation', and ever ready throughout his long life to defend the old ways. Even to make the final sacrifice.

Cut.

This was '72. Ominous times. The flowers of the Sixties faded. The long trough of the new decade yawning. The Irish trouble. And the sense of a new, barbarous world encroaching, a world no longer keeping to its former demarcations, former protocol. Bombs going off in airports, embassies, shopping centres, homes.

You could say they were successful: they eliminated their target. You could say they miscalculated: they erected a monument.

People want stories. They don't want facts. Even journalists say 'story' when they mean 'event'. Of the news photo they say: Every picture tells a story – worth two columns of words. But supposing it doesn't tell a story? Supposing it shows only un-accommodatable fact? Supposing it shows the point at which the story breaks down. The point at which narrative goes dumb.

No art. Just straight photography. Avoid beauty, composition, statements, symbols, eloquence, rhetoric, decorum, taste. All that is painting. But just hold open the shutter when the world wants to close its eyes.

Brian Patterson, at his Fleet Street desk, was the first to get hold of me, less than an hour after the story 'broke'. Even got through somehow on that red-hot Hyfield number. Behind the confidential, I'm-talking-to-you-as-a-friend voice, I could hear journalistic excitement mixed with journalistic frustration (on a *Monday* of all days – and this was a Sunday paper).

'You were there when it happened – is that right?'

'Yes. Yes.'

'God, I'm sorry. What can I say?'

'It's okay.'

'You weren't hurt?'

'No.'

'Sophie?'

'Shock. Just shock. They've taken her to hospital. Shock.'

'Look, Harry – I – Do you want to cover this one?'

All through that day, that evening, the next day and the next: phone calls, questions, propositions. 'Mr Beech, can you describe for us . . .?'; 'Mr Beech, what are your feelings at this moment?'; 'Mr Beech, as a distinguished news photographer, who has . . .'; 'You were actually just about to leave for Belfast, is that true?'; 'What were the last words that . . .?'; 'We understand that your daughter . . .'; 'Harry? Is that you, Harry? We're putting together this two-minute piece. Your father's life. We wondered if you had any material. You know, family photos . . .'; 'Only a few words – a son's tribute . . .'; 'So you and he were not always . . .'; 'What we want, Harry, is some personal stuff. You know, the real man, the inside story . . .'

No comment. No comment. No. And no again. There was always the same tone of almost indignant surprise, of veiled reproach. But you were there, weren't you? A big story, and you're right in the middle of it. You're Harry Beech, aren't you? The true pro. Stop at nothing. Just because –

That first swarm of photographers outside the gates at Hyfield, when Joe and I returned in the police car from the hospital, took me totally unawares. I who had stood – how many times, in the early days? – waiting for cars, lunging forward as they swung by. The flash-bulbs, like pistol shots. The faces. Hey, Harry – how come you're there on the inside looking out. Looking at us.

No, I don't want to cover it. You're asking the wrong man. The man you should be talking to – if you can get him between discreet calls from Whitehall – is Frank Irving. Acting

93

Chairman. He'll give you all you want to know. Full story. Slip in, while you're at it, a few direct questions about BMC, about arms trade ethics. No? Too underhand, too 'unpatriotic', under the circumstances? Unlike asking a son to –

One of Frank's first acts as duly appointed Chairman: to commission a bronze bust, larger than life-size, to be placed on a plinth in the main foyer of the office. A bust, or rather head only, to avoid the problem of artificially representing an artificial arm.

A hero's death. A martyr's death.

(And that extra, poignant touch. The chauffeur. A cameo part. Sacrifice within sacrifice.)

No, I'm not covering it.

Because I'd already covered it. Already been the true, unflinching, the ultimate pro.

SOPHIE

—

Darling Doctor K, we mustn't go on meeting like this. Here in your darkened room, on your couch, with my mind all undressed. People might talk. People might tell.

It was supposed to be a little, brief, therapeutic fling, wasn't it? A few intimate and secret sessions with you, then back to normality again, all the better for it. Back to being the loving wife and mother I used to dream once upon a time that I was.

But it's getting to be serious, you and me. It's getting to be a regular thing.

I kiss him goodbye in the morning. He says: You're seeing Doctor Klein today? I say, Yes, and he kisses me again, as if it's my work-out at the gym day or my special treat for being a good girl day. Then I take the kids to school, then I come on over the river and tell you things I've never told him. Tell you, a little, dry, elegant, elfin man, who I don't know a thing about and I only met three months ago, what I'd never tell him. Though I've known him for sixteen years, and once we used to fuck like mad things all round that place we went to for weekends on Poros. We used to eat these big red chunks of water-melon – *karpouzia* – naked, so the juice ran all down. Then he wasn't eating the water-melon, he was eating me.

95

See what I mean? I could be trying to come on to you, couldn't I? Telling you things like that.

It could be some deal, I guess. An arrangement, a conscience-salver. (He pays!) Because really he's screwing his secretary, down there on Sixth, every other evening. But I know he's not. Because that's not Joe. And even if he were, I'd know, I'd smell it on him. So why doesn't he smell it on me? Smell Nick the plumber. And Dean the insurance agent. And Jerry the just-divorced husband of Karen Sherman. Because he isn't like that. He doesn't have that sort of sensitive nose. Or eye. Or memory. A toy gun is just a toy gun.

And, besides, they were just cheap, quick, mindless screws, to make me forget I was anybody, to make me think I was nobody.

Not like you and me.

There's always hypnosis. Isn't that a technique they use? We haven't tried that. Oh yes, I'd gladly let you send me sweetly to sleep. Happily let you probe and pry just as you wished while I lay back in a state of unresisting, unremembering uncon-sciousness. What's the matter? Don't you trust me? What do you think I'll do? Leap up, start beating on the door and shout, Rape! Rape!

But it's okay. It's I who trust you! You're cool, you're pro-fessional, your credentials are good. I've got to be perfectly frank and co-operative with you and hold nothing back, and if I don't drop my psychic panties like a sensible girl, how can you help me? You're neutral, you're scientifically detached, I'm safe in your hands. And it doesn't matter what I say, does it, it won't bring a blush to those lightly tanned cheeks, or alternatively give you unprofessional ideas?

You've got it, Doctor K. Older men. Got it in one. I guess it was obvious from the start. I guess you know all the signs, all the symptoms. I've got this thing about older men. Little old wise men who know it all. And little kids, little twins, who'll

96

have to be told it all. In between it's just foraging, isn't it? Just make and mend and *sauve qui peut* and a little rough stuff thrown in. Isn't that so?

And you're a *small* man, of course! That figures. I mean, you're not a big, Big man. No disrespect. You don't *tower*, you don't *threaten*. A strong wind would blow you over, wouldn't it? But it wouldn't actually *ruffle* you either. You know, I thought at first: O-oh, he's a *small* guy. They're always the worst. Watch it, Sophie, this could be your classic shrink – a crackpot in disguise. But your smallness is like a kind of distillation. It's as though you were boiled down at some time, or slowly over the years, so there's nothing spare or unnecessary or untidy about you. 'Small,' you said. 'It's my name. "Klein" means "small". Small by name and small by nature. Just a small man in a big world, Sophie.' Holding up those little hands, as if you'd never use a weapon. It was the first thing you ever said about *yourself*.

About the only damn thing, fuck you.

Ha! – I should tell you my fantasies, right? Oh please, let me. I'd like to pick you up – you're so neat and light – and put you in the bath-tub. Really. Just like I do with Tim and Paul. I still do. Though it's getting near the knuckle. Sponge them down. Run the soap round their little dormant cocks. Oh, pardon me, I didn't mean to imply – (Mother *you*? You?) I don't think of you without your clothes on. Do you think of me without my clothes on? I don't think of your cock. But I bet it's cute and toothsome.

I still do it. But I won't for much longer, will I? They'll shut the bathroom door on me. Facts of life. I'll open it and they'll have slipped through the window, out into the world.

I wanted a private life, that's all. From then on. A simple, comfy, domestic life. But it's all dissolving.

Warm and steamy and pink-smelling. A cocoon.

Put one of those sweet hands there again. I mean here, on my

97

forehead. (But put it anywhere you like, anywhere you like.) You know, when you do that, just that, it's better than anything. Better than all your clever words, surrogate amnesia and professional letters after your name. A cool, calm, neutral hand on my brow. Worth eighty dollars an hour, just for that. And why can't Joe do that? That's just what he wants to *be*: a calm, firm, comforting hand on my brow. But he can't do it. And I don't want him to do it.

And so he pays for you! For us!

Keep your hands there. Tell me I'm attractive. Say: Sophie, you're an attractive woman. You're a beautiful lady. That's how I'll always see her, you know. Clear, fresh, always. On the lawn, under the sun umbrella. Her big black eyes, laughing lips. Making Grandad laugh. One strap of her summer dress falling over her lovely olive shoulder. That's how I always wanted to be. To make him happy too. To be like her in his eyes. That last time, on the terrace, with the glasses of champagne . . .

Sure, I'll tell you anything. I'll turn myself inside out for you. Self-respect and modesty haven't exactly been my forte just recently. You watch, you sit back and enjoy the show. It must be good to be you. It must be great to be you.

Should've ended, shouldn't it? Should've split before it got too involved. Goodbye Sophie – you're your own woman now. But it's gone on, hasn't it? (As long as you like, Sophie, as long as you want.) And it's going to go on. Because you see – yes, I really do have something to tell you – he's written this letter. Harry has written this letter. And you'll never guess, you won't believe, what it says.

I haven't shown it to Joe. I haven't told him I've got it. Because I think if he knew I'd heard from Harry, he'd be, I don't know – angry? Hurt? Afraid? And if he knew that I wanted – If he knew that, after all, I really wanted – Then I think he'd know too: that I don't – Haven't for years. Not any more.

He's going to get married. He's going to get fucking *married*. To some fucking *girl*. And he wants me to – He'd like me – He wants me.

HARRY

—

Small worlds. Big worlds. The one can eclipse the other. When the moon blots out the sun and makes the world go dark, it isn't because the moon is bigger than the sun.

When I went to Nuremberg in 1946 to cover the end of the war trials, on my first foreign assignment as a fledgling news photographer, I was looking, as my employers were looking, as the whole world was looking, for monsters. Goering, Hess, Keitel, von Ribbentrop . . . Capture in their faces the obscenity of their crimes, capture in their eyes the death of millions, capture in the furrows of their brows the enormity of their guilt. Jodl, Sauckel, Kaltenbrunner . . .

But I didn't find monsters. I found this collection of dull, nondescript, headphoned men, thin and pale from months in prison, with the faces of people in waiting rooms or people co-opted into some tedious, routine task. Only Goering rose – if this is the right phrase – to the occasion, and with a smart line in sarcasm and courtroom repartee, played the part of stage villain. But that too was wrong. As if we should get to love him, be amused by him. As if he should become some celebrity, a story-book figure, and we would say: We forget the others, but that Goering, now he was a character.

Where was the horror? And where was the sense of the suspended weight of the sword of History, which, if it should have hung over any point on earth in September 1946, should have hung over that courthouse in Nuremberg. Beneath the rows of white-helmeted military police, the lawyers and officials fidgeted in their seats, scratched their chins, looked at watches, stifled yawns. The testimonies, the evidence, the statistics that must have been, when the trial opened, the object of terrible attention, were repeated now, almost a year later, with a kind of laborious matter-of-factness. Yes, we have heard all this before, but shall we go through it once again, try to approach it from a fresh angle?

I thought: So what is there to capture? And then I realized. It is this ordinariness I must capture. This terrible ordinariness. The fact of this ordinariness. I must show that monsters do not belong to comfortable tales. That the worst things are perpetrated by people no one would pick out from a crowd.

Rosenberg, being marched from prison to courthouse. He squints, he seems distracted. He looks like a man with a headache, a morning hangover, that's all. He has nicked himself shaving.

People cannot comprehend large numbers or great extremes. They cannot comprehend a thousand deaths, or routine atrocity, or the fact that there are situations – they arise and spread so quickly – in which life becomes suddenly so cheap that it is worth next to nothing, less than nothing, and killing is as casual as being killed. These things are pushed to the remote borders of the mind, where perhaps they will be wafted into someone else's territory. But they can contemplate one death, or one life. Or a handful of deaths or a handful of lives. And they watch, almost with glad relief, when the unthinkable facts of a decade are unloaded on to the figures of twenty-one men who are placed, as it were, on a stage with the entire world as audience, and the whole thing takes on the solemnized aspect of ritual.

Nothing is more edifying than a courtroom drama. Nothing is more conscience-cleansing than an exhibition of culprits. Nothing is more cathartic than the conversion of fact into fable.

Save of course that no fable, no drama can sustain itself indefinitely. By the eighth or ninth month of the Nuremberg War Trial the audience had wearied. They felt free to let their attention wander. But now, in September 1946, drama was returning to what seemed to have descended into mere bureaucracy. Judgement was nigh, the denouement was due.

Outside the courtroom, in the autumn sunshine, the rubble of Nuremberg was still being cleared. Two years before in the calm of an Air Force Intelligence establishment I had gazed on frozen, monochrome images of Nuremberg being destroyed from the air. The city that was progressively laid waste right up until the early months of '45 was the old medieval capital of Franconia, a city of churches, towers, merchants and craftsmen – clock-makers, gold-beaters, silversmiths. Since 1946 this intricate product of the centuries has been rebuilt. It is not real, of course. It is a modern reconstruction, but it has been painstakingly done – so I am told – as if to re-conjure a world before certain irreversible historical events had happened. Now, Nuremberg is one of the chief tourist towns of Germany. People go for these picturesque reconstructions, mixed with genuine remnants of the old, for the fairy-tale spires and gables. The one-time site of Nazi rallies and the scene of the War Trials are of secondary interest.

After the executions were carried out in the prison gymnasium in the early morning of October 16th, I took photos of the crowd which had gathered in the first light of day outside the prison walls. It consisted of members of the Allied occupying forces and administration, but among them were a few, less assertive, German faces. They were gathered to experience a momentous communal thrill which they felt, plainly,

103

was theirs by right and which would be intensified, as if by some physical charge, by their proximity to its source. They were waiting for some sign, some revelation, a display of corpses, perhaps, at which they might cheer and raise their fists; and their faces wore a look of murderous exultation. These too were the faces of ordinary people.

Eleven were condemned and seven received prison sentences. Of the condemned, only Goering, whose defence had been – is this the right word? – so spirited, played a final trick on his audience by swallowing concealed poison. It is said that there was horse-trading amongst the Allied nations as to who should die. It is also said that the executioner deliberately bungled the hangings, so that some, at least, of those who died, died slowly and horribly. Was this a crime against humanity?

I don't recall now where they had flown that night. Conceivably, it was Nuremberg. In any case I hadn't flown with them (and I was glad of that). But I was taking shots of the planes as they returned at dawn. For one of the Lancs things had gone badly – or not so badly, depending on how you look at it, since the plane got back, as others didn't, and all save two of the crew were unharmed. They were transferring the pilot from the cockpit to the ambulance, and I should have been stopped, perhaps, from coming so close. But (I would discover this later over and over again) people don't stop you. They don't, as a rule, make a grab for your camera, or for you. They are too busy, too caught up. You are just another mad part of the scene. It's afterwards that they say: Did you see?! That bastard with the camera!

The pilot was supported in a cradle formed by the joined arms of two ambulance crew who were walking him from the plane. His arms were round their necks and he was held in a sort of jammed foetal position, as if his knees couldn't be prized from his abdomen. His lips were curled back and his teeth clamped together, so he looked like some terrible parody of a man straining to void his bowels. He had flown back from Germany and landed his aircraft with a cannon shell up his arse, and his face was green with the pain.

I took three, four pictures, which the Air Ministry promptly impounded, these not being the sort of pictures they had in mind (even if they were, according to my brief, 'authentic visual records of the air war'). But several years later they released them, and one of them is included in *Aftermaths*, in the first section called 'Bombers 1945' (it is captioned simply 'Lancaster pilot' with the name of the base and the date), and became regarded as one of my 'famous' early shots.

That pilot was awarded, posthumously, the D.F.C. for his act of heroism in bringing back his plane and crew. When you look at the photo you do not think, I think, of heroism. You think of pain and absurdity. But your mind focuses on that agonized young airman in an act of compassionate concentration that it would be sacrilegious to call sentimental. You think of personal things. You wonder who he was. You imagine his home somewhere, his parents, his girl. You think of him as an unsuspecting schoolboy. You do not think – it would seem almost blasphemous to do so – of the many hundreds of men, women and children who were killed or maimed as a result of the raid in which this young pilot took part. You do not think of the bombs stored in the bomb-bay of the now emptied and shot-up plane in the background. Nor would you think (assuming you were told the nature of the pilot's fatal wound) of the cannon shell, that particular cannon shell, amongst so many cannon shells. How it must have been turned out, one of millions, in some mid-European works. How it must have passed through the hands of a munitions worker, a girl in a mob-cap, imagine. Whether she had relatives who had been killed in air raids. Whether she could have conceivably guessed the final resting place of that shell. Whether she ever thought of where those shells it was her business to send on their way might end up. Surely she did, but then there were so many shells: to think of them all, impossible; to think of one, pointless. But you stare fixedly at this suffering figure, picked out from the random carnage of war, destined not only for a posthumous medal but also – But then something rebels against your concentration, something undermines the very purity of your pity. Also to be the object of photographic contemplation.

'An act of heroism' suggests always, if only at first, something glamorous and emblematic: a handsome face turned to some dangerous prospect. We say of certain things that they are not only done but must be seen to be done. We say this, for example, of Justice. When that dead pilot was awarded the D.F.C., you could say that heroism was seen to be done. This is not to suggest there was no actual heroism, but the actual heroism may have been of a quite different kind from that which went recognized. After all (but again this seems almost blasphemous), what choice did he have? Was it as though he willed his life to culminate in an act, and that particular act, of heroism? And, at the terrible moment, what *else* could he do, with a parcel of hot metal up his rectum and a dead flight engineer and a damaged aircraft? Appeal to some hidden power and say: Wake me out of this dream?

When I took that photograph I thought to myself, if not in so many words: Let this have no aesthetic content, let this be only like it is, in the middle of things. Since I knew already that photos taken in even the most chaotic circumstances can acquire, lifted from the mad flow of events, a perverse formality and poise. I thought this as I took the picture. I did not think of the pilot. Was this an act of inhumanity?

The two orderlies are staggering slightly. It is like some joke version of the exhausted athlete being carried in triumph. One second please, face the camera please (but his eyes were shut to the world), to record your moment of glory.

106

I half hid behind the swung-open ambulance door, then stepped out and clicked.

My first picture of a dying man.

Until I went to Nuremberg in '46 I had not seen, at ground level, any of the damage done to Germany. I was not, though I might easily have been, amongst those photographers specifically despatched to record the progress of Liberation and the evidence of defeat. Nor was I amongst those first on the scene, who would never forget being present, when the camps at Buchenwald, Belsen and elsewhere were opened. But a future, now late colleague of mine, Bill Cochrane, was. Our careers evolved along similar lines, since Bill at the time was a War Office photographer, just as I was accredited to the Air Ministry. Some of Bill's photographs were used in the Allies' propaganda campaign of post-war 'enlightenment' and de-Nazification, others found their way into the mass of documentation submitted to the Nuremberg prosecutors.

Seeing is believing and certain things must be seen to have been done. Without the camera the world might start to disbelieve. At the newly liberated camps local civilians were made to file past the emaciated corpses in order to witness facts of which, despite their proximity, they had no greater knowledge than the newly arrived Allies. There is a photo of Bill's showing this procedure taking place. A man is looking at something near his feet, with an expression of confusion on his face. You cannot tell if the confusion is the result of what he is looking at or the knowledge that he is being photographed.

Which is worse: to have to look at piles of corpses? Or to photograph people looking at piles of corpses? Would Bill have taken this photo if he were not ordered to do so? Was it an act of inhumanity?

Bill Cochrane was killed in the Congo in '63, trying to take pictures of an ambush when he had already been hit in the leg. His death itself became a minor news item, there was a half-column report, a brief obituary, and I was asked to attend a memorial service at St Bride's. Posthumous honours came his way. Should journalists receive medals and citations? For courage and sacrifice in the service of truth? Is it truth they are after, or are they just trying to be heroes?

Bill and I worked together for a while on the same paper. He used to tell a story about when he was at Nordhausen, the first of the camps he witnessed. He had not known then that he would later become a professional news photographer or whether he wanted to be one. Before the corpses were removed he deliberately went to look at them, because he thought he should do so without the protection, as it were, of his camera. He found himself virtually alone beside a row of bodies – people were staying clear because of the terrible smell – but while he was standing there an American corporal approached from the other end of the row. Bill used to say that the corporal's uniform looked particularly new and pressed and his face clean and fresh, as if he had just stepped off the troop plane, but I wondered if this was Bill's embellishment. The G.I. was approaching the corpses with a handkerchief held over his nose and mouth, but he also had a camera round his neck – his own camera, new-looking – and he started to take pictures. He would wrench his hand from his face, raise the camera and repeat, 'Oh my God, oh my God,' apparently not noticing Bill. Bill said it was like some parody of the determined sightseer desperate to take snaps for the folks back home. He wondered whether without the camera the corporal could have got so near. Or whether he needed, as if to convince himself, the future proof of what his own eyes were seeing.

But the point of the story is that in his agitation the American had forgotten to take the lens-cap from his camera. Bill said he could have gone up to him and told him. He could have made that decision. But he didn't.

SOPHIE

———

How can I tell, Doctor K? Tell me how to tell it. People say: 'It was all over in an instant' or 'It happened so quickly.' But it isn't like that. Something happens to time. Something happens to normality. A hole gets blasted in it. A hole with no bottom to it. So what is over in an instant just goes on happening. It happens in long slow-motion. And then it just keeps on happening. So that afterwards, when I was some place else, here in New York, three thousand miles away, it wasn't afterwards or some other place, I was still there, on the terrace at Hyfield, standing, frozen, as if I might never move again, with that strange noise in my ears, the noise of absolute silence. Couldn't even hear Mrs Keane screaming. Apparently she was screaming, her mouth was wide open. Only the voice in my head, like the distant voice down a telephone, which was saying: Something terrible has happened. Is happening. Is happening.

Because you don't believe it. You don't believe that one moment – Then the next – Because you don't believe it can have happened. So it goes on happening. Till you believe it. How can I tell you what I don't believe? What do you want me to say? I was there. Heard. Saw. On the spot. How does that help?

And what am I trying to tell you, anyway? That on an April morning ten years ago, my grandfather was blown up by terrorists, along with his chauffeur and a Daimler. And that if I hadn't been standing there on the terrace, about to sit down with the cup of coffee Mrs Keane had brought, and thinking, Now I will talk to Harry – if I'd said goodbye to Grandad at the front porch and not on the terrace ('Goodbye,' he said, 'no, stay here, sit down,' like a husband who thinks that even a newly pregnant woman shouldn't move) – then I might – Too.

Goodbye. A kiss. Another sixty seconds –

And if Harry hadn't been up in the rear bedroom, packing his things – And if Mrs Keane hadn't just stepped from the kitchen, with a fresh tray of coffee –

But you know all that. Or you can look it up. Do you do your homework, Doctor K? 'Lucky escape of Harry Beech and his Daughter': that was how the newspapers put it, mentioning Mrs Keane only as an afterthought. Lucky escape! And then of course the pictures. The 'gruesome' pictures. Wreckage 'littering the once immaculate lawn'. Policemen sifting. And the newsreels and telerecordings. Mr and Mrs Carmichael leaving the hospital. (Can you describe, Mrs Carmichael, can you describe, exactly?) Harry Beech arriving at Hyfield in a police car. He looks like a criminal. 'This very morning, by grim irony, Mr Beech was about to leave for Northern Ireland.'

It's all there. It was all news, public knowledge. What more can I say? Except how it really –

By grim irony.

You see, I wanted to talk to him alone. I wanted to sit there with him on the terrace, just like I'd sat with Grandad, and talk. About me and Joe. And America and Hyfield. About homes and families (homes and families!). He had an hour or more before he had to leave for his plane. I think I even said to him, Go and pack your things, then let's talk. I wanted to say to him, When did we last talk together, really talk, you and I? Yes,

yes, I know you are going off, again, to Northern Ireland this time, and that is far more important of course than any piffling bit of news I can give you, like the fact that I am pregnant. But I am going to be a mother. Doesn't that remind you of being a father?

But.

He must have looked out of the rear bedroom window. Seen us on the terrace: the coffee things scattered over the paving, Mrs Keane screaming her head off without making a single sound. Then he must have gone through to the front landing.

Or maybe he didn't even bother to check where we were.

How long did I stand, petrified on the terrace? You don't consult a stop-watch, you don't have a tape-measure. You don't say: Let's make an objective – I went into the house. The way you walk in dreams. It wasn't a house any more. A fog of dust and smoke. Perhaps I was glad of that fog. Glass. Broken things. I didn't believe it. A hub-cap lying in the hall. The front door flung at the foot of the stairs. I went out where the front door wasn't.

Little scattered fires all over the lawn.

What do you want, an exact description? I saw what you see when a bomb has gone off in a car with two people in it. Enough? The police say, Have you told us everything? You say, Isn't that enough? They say, Can you remember anything else? The police are a bit like you, Doctor K. Only less cute.

He was leaning out of the upstairs window. I don't know why I looked up. Because I saw him move? Because looking up, looking away, was better than – He was leaning out of the upstairs window. Or rather, where the window had been.

You see, that's when I believed. That's when I knew it's all one territory and everywhere, everywhere can be a target and there aren't any safe, separate places any more. I've never told anyone. I've kept so quiet about it that sometimes I actually think it was – what would you call it? – a 'hallucination under

111

extreme stress'. I saw him first, then he saw me. He was like a man caught sleep-walking, not knowing how he could be doing what he was doing, as if it were all part of some deep, ingrained reflex. But just for a moment I saw this look on his face of deadly concentration. He hadn't seen me first because he'd been looking elsewhere, and his eyes had been jammed up against a camera.

HARRY

Privacy! That was the word that was always flung at me!

The photograph, not the photographer. No autobiography, please. And no glamour, definitely no glamour.

Only once, in the autumn of '66, when Sophie was abroad (was that significant?), did I consent to present myself as the subject – or should I say object? – of media scrutiny. I still remember the studio lights, those beige studio chairs, the clip-on microphone with the wire that ran up my sleeve, and the feeling that I had only myself to blame – for surrendering to my publisher's coercion (this was the year of *Aftermaths*) and (I confess it) to the inducements of flattery. Since the lead-in, at least, to this twenty-five-minute late-night slot, was cheerily declaring: 'Already a growing legend among news photo-graphers . . .' If it was also ominously stating its terms: 'But what of the man behind the camera? The mind behind the lens . . . ?'

I wore a dark-grey suit and a reticent tie. To look as an-onymous and as much like an accountant as possible. To avoid the bush-jacket image. But under the studio lights I started to sweat.

I still hear that young and sure-voiced interviewer explaining to our invisible audience with the air of an amateur psycho-logist, that I came from 'privileged circumstances' (public school, Oxford, family business) but had 'turned my back on all that' for the rigours of news photography. Furthermore, that while my father was the head of an arms company (BMC spelling, for those who weren't aware in these days of burgeoning flower-power: 'Beech Munitions Company') and was a distinguished former soldier, I had 'specialized' in photo-graphs depicting the evils of war.

Had rebellion and protest been factors in my career?

I said I did not see myself as a professional rebel. I saw myself as an observer, a visual reporter. I disliked the word 'specialized', since I had photographed many other things beside wars.

My interviewer smiled as if we could now relax. He had established a disputatious tone. This would be good TV.

If not rebellion, then emulation perhaps? If we could stick with war for a while. (We stuck with war for most of the programme.) My father was a holder of the v.c. and a hero of the First War, and a fair proportion (let's say) of my work might be described as 'front-line' photography – pictures that must have taken some nerve (he gave the word a subtle stress) to take.

I said that it took a good deal less nerve to photograph many of the situations I had photographed than to be an active and involuntary participant of those situations. That a large part of a photo-journalist's work was spent on the relative periphery of events or in routine concerns (transport, communication, the protection of one's gear). That you went into things with the knowledge that you could soon pull out (press men also were 'privileged'). Of course, you were sometimes inescapably caught up, but then it wasn't a case of heroics, just of dedication to the job.

What were my most hazardous assignments? Had I had any

114

close calls? Had anyone tried to smash my camera, seize my film? Etc. Etc.

I told two half-prepared anecdotes (Algiers, '61; Stanleyville, '64) and one (poor) joke: my most dangerous assignment had been to photograph the film actress D— in a New York hotel, the day after her live-theatre come-back had been unanimously panned by the critics. Couldn't we get back to the photographs themselves?

Of course. Did I think there were any limitations to 'dedication to the job'?

That needed explaining.

Flash on to screen, while interviewer speaks, photograph of Vietnamese woman, with contorted face, holding a blood-soaked child.

'This photo of a grieving mother, included in your *Aftermaths* collection, appeared, in full colour, in millions of Sunday newspapers shortly after the event it records. Mr Beech, your work has been much praised – even if praise may not be your object. But many people take exception to it. They would say that you invade privacy.'

He leant back expectantly in his chair.

(Later, I could not help following that young man's career, through the echelons of TV, in the Sixties and Seventies. At the end of our twenty-five minutes, as the credits rolled and we were off the air, he said, without a trace of innuendo, 'That was tremendous! Really *good!*' and proffered his copy of *Aftermaths* for signing.)

I said that in the case of that particular photo, privacy was hardly an issue. The woman's village had just been destroyed by American rockets. She was by no means the only grieving mother. I was by no means the only onlooker. I imagined the fact that her grief was on view was the least important element of it.

(Cut from talking head back to photo: close in on central image.)

115

Frankly, I found the idea of 'invaded privacy' curiously misplaced. Since the suffering observed in my photographs was frequently the result of quite literal and traumatic invasions. When civilian homes were bombed or communities forced into refugeedom, or even when a soldier was conscripted into a war he did not understand, this was a theft of privacy of much greater significance than any taking of a photo. In my experience, privacy was a notion that in fact meant little to a great number of people in the world, because they did not possess it or had little chance of keeping it. It was – I paused over the word – a privilege of the West. A notion particularly dear to the English. *Whose* privacy were we talking about anyway? The privacy of the people in my photographs or the privacy of Sunday-morning newspaper readers wanting to enjoy their breakfasts?

Cut to Ia Drang valley, South Vietnam, November '65. Supine G.I., encircled by two anguished buddies (helmets removed: dangled crucifix just visible) and medic with drip-pack. (Strong breeze blows across group: helicopter rotors, out of picture.)

Cut to north-eastern Congo, October '64. Three prisoners squatting on ground beneath banana-leaf canopy, hands bound behind backs and necks linked with a rope. A guard or captor stands behind them in jungle camouflage fatigues, holding an automatic rifle. The guard is burly and erect and totally absorbed for the moment with having his picture taken. He beams at the camera, like a jovial stall-holder. The prisoners, clad only in shorts and singlets, are also facing the camera, but they are wearing blindfolds.

Cut to Birmingham, Alabama, September '63. Bare interior, with family group. A listless-looking man lies, eyeing camera, on a mattress, rear of picture. A bulky woman, centre picture, in ragged cotton shift, arranges the hair of a second female figure who sits on an upturned crate and is in garish contrast

116

to her surroundings. She is got up in the costume of a whore: tight fake-satin dress, high heels, heavy lipstick, piled-up hair. This superficially makes her look older than she is, but at the same time accentuates her actual youth. You can tell from the angularity of her body she can be no more than twelve.

While these pictures appeared in quick (too quick) succession on the screen, they were simultaneously displayed by back projector behind us in the studio. As the first appeared, my interviewer swivelled his chair round, thumb and forefinger to his chin, in an exaggerated gesture of attention, leaving me to do likewise or to be caught briefly looking abandoned and awkward. (This too was a picture!) Before the third image disappeared and when we were once more on camera, he swivelled back again, with equal studiedness, catching the camera's eye.

'But do you not often feel, when taking your photographs, like an intruder?'

Yes, I did often feel that. Precisely that. But this struck me as being in the nature of photography itself, especially of news photography. You could not photograph the news by prior arrangement. The great value of photography was its actuality, its lack of prejudicial tact, its very power of intrusion. This could not be achieved by knocking at the door first.

'A sort of shock tactics?'

'I wouldn't say that.'

'But you intend to shock. You set out to do that?'

'I don't have intentions. I don't engineer effects. If my pictures shock it is because their subject-matter shocks.'

'But you select the subject-matter. Isn't that a kind of engineering?'

'I'm a news photographer. I can't select the news.'

'But would you say then that there is no personal element in your work. Nothing of yourself. No bit of Harry Beech?'

117

'The point of a photograph isn't to portray the photographer. If someone looks at a photo of mine and they think of me, the photographer, then I'd say that that photograph has failed.'

Cut to Kyrenia, northern Cyprus, April '64 (and hold on back projection). Interior scene after mortar attack. A teenage boy crouches by a lacerated victim, but at the moment of the photograph his head has swung imploringly round, without yet registering (the last thing he has expected) the camera. His face is a blurred scream for help.

'But isn't that – if you'll forgive me – just how many people do respond to your photos. They think: What makes a man take a picture like this?'

There were always in those days those two kinds of reaction. Either I was this new type of hero, this okay type of hero, a hero without a gun, without a weapon, but flinching at nothing to bring back the truth. Or (the majority?) there was only one thought: What kind of freak, what kind of sicko stands in front of the maimed and dying and desperate, and calmly (calmly! Stands!) snaps their photograph? And what kind of warped mentality *voluntarily* sets out looking for such pictures in the first place?

A defence mechanism, of course. Whip the messenger because of the news.

And just look what happens in the spring of 1972 when that news that he has been pursuing for over fifteen years finally catches up with *him*? He stands off-stage, like a gormless understudy. His shady mock-heroics pale before the real, the true – the ultimate – stuff of his father. And what's more to the point, almost overnight, it seems, he abandons photography. Like some confession of guilt. Leaves the field and disappears from the world.

So, wasn't that quits? No? Not only the subversive but the

118

reneger too? So what did they want? That for the sake of integrity, I should have snapped my own father's death?

People look for motives, reasons (as a last resort, try the Oedipus Complex), things to explain things away. Never mind the cause if the effect failed, never mind the effect if the cause can be discredited. A personal thing, you see. A psychological thing. He was a bit of a case. So we don't have to take seriously those grim souvenirs he brought back from far-off places.

Just an observer! Just an eye behind a lens!

Have you heard the one about the white-coated scientist? (Or, say, impartial observer, or, say, photographer?) He came along once upon a time and said, Now, at last, I can show you how the world really is. Very impressive, very persuasive. Until someone said, Hold on just a second – the fact that you're standing there looking at it is changing the way the world is anyway. If you're going to tell us how things are, then maybe we should start with you.

Have you noticed how the world has changed? It's become this vast display of evidence, this exhibition of recorded data, this continuously running movie.

The problem is what you don't see. The problem is your field of vision. (A picture of the whole world!) The problem is selection (true, Mr Interviewer), the frame, the separation of the image from the thing. The extraction of the world from the world. The problem is where and how you draw the line. (Sometimes it's simple: Hold those shots of the African refugees, we need the half-page for the airline ad.)

There is a picture of mine (one of the 'famous photos') of a marine throwing a grenade at Hoi An. His right arm is stretched back, his whole body flexed, beneath the helmet you can see the profile of a handsome face. It's pure Greek statue, pure Hollywood, pure charisma. And it's how it was. It must have been. Because the camera showed it. A second later, that marine took a round in the chest and I took two more shots and then some more as they got him clear. I wanted the whole sequence to be printed. But you can guess – you know – which single shot they took. This was '65. And that picture got syndicated everywhere, and even got transferred, with or without my knowledge, but never with my consent, on to posters, book-jackets, propaganda hand-outs, even T-shirts, till no one remembered any more, if they had ever known, that this was a picture of a real man, who'd died seconds afterwards, or wondered who he was or what small town in the Mid-West he came from (it was Bloomington, Indiana), or ever considered – it was an image, it was *there* – that someone must have taken the original pic.

What is a photograph? It's an object. It's something defined, with an edge. You can pick it up, look at it, like a pebble from a beach, like a lump of rock chipped from the moon. You can put it here or there, in an album, on a mantelpiece, in a newspaper, in a book. A long time after the event it is still there, and when you look at it you shut out everything else. It becomes an icon, a totem, a curio. A photo is a piece of reality? A fragment of the truth?

I am sixty-four years old, and the picture looms before me, exquisitely framed, of building my life round a beautiful girl of twenty-three.

When I was nine or ten or so I used to make the journey several times a year between my home and my prep school, thirty miles away in Hampshire. I would be driven to Dorking station. The chauffeur in those days was called Beatty, and the car, believe it or not, was a Lanchester 21. The porter would take my bags and I would give him the coins that Dad had given me to give him, and he would touch his cap as if he were studiously playing the character of a porter. Then I would get a train, changing at Guildford, to Petersfield.

It never occurred to me that there must be sons of parents living in London who were dispatched to boarding schools in Surrey, near Dorking, or that a whole system of English education was based on the removal of the young to, at least, the next county.

I should have found the outward journeys, the back-to-school journeys, the more wretched. But I could never have said which was worse, going to school or going home, because I dreaded both places. The two dreads would sometimes cancel themselves out into a sort of numb suspension, so that I would say to myself: You belong nowhere. Or rather: *This* is the only place you belong – this transit region, this in-between space.

I would sit with my face to the window while the damp Surrey fields slid by, and think: All you are is your eyes, all there is is in your eyes, your vision is you. And there was a corollary to this which if I couldn't formulate I could feel. If you exist in your vision, then nothing can hurt you, you need never be frightened of anything.

If you talk to news photographers who from time to time will put themselves in the most dangerous situations or amidst the most terrible scenes in order to get their pictures, they will describe a similar sensation. The camera seems to make them invisible, invulnerable, incorporeal. They are like those immortal gods and goddesses who flitted unharmed round the plain at Troy. This heady sense of immunity will even compel them, over and above their obligations as journalists, to keep on visiting these zones of danger. Hey, don't shoot me, don't blame me. I'm only here for the photograph.

This is, of course, an illusion. It didn't stop Bill Cochrane, amongst others, from being killed with his camera in his hand. But it is a potent illusion, which exists even in the most amateur and innocuous forms of photography, and perhaps it is why the photo, the film, which once people existed entirely without,

121

has become almost a necessity of life. A photo is a reprieve, an act of suspension, a charm. If you see something terrible or wonderful, that you can't take in or focus your feelings for – a battlefield, the Taj Mahal, the woman with whom you think you are falling in love – take a picture of it, hold the camera to it. Look again when it's safe. I have always loved flying.

SOPHIE

How are your classics, Doctor K? Have you brushed up on your Homer lately? It's strange, I might never have been interested. All those books up there in the study. Fifty years old, the spines faded; but so many of them, inside, scarcely used, the relics of a career that never happened. And the plaster busts. Let me see if I can remember: Homer, Pericles, Virgil, Cicero. Two with beards and two without. And all with blind, white eyes. I might never have been interested, I might have thought of that room just as it always seemed, a place somehow you didn't *go*, if it wasn't that one day – don't ask me how old I was, eleven, twelve – I had suddenly thought: Greek! Greece! Maybe it was a way back to *her*.

He never touched the books. Just went up there sometimes to write letters at the desk, which was always kept locked. I remember asking him, and he said, 'Oh, Greek and Latin. Gods and heroes, all that rot.' I remember him saying that. 'All that rot'. So I don't know why he kept them there, for Mrs Keane to dust. Unless it was just to preserve the sense of a life that might have been. As if, had Uncle Edward, in some fantastic way, suddenly shown up, Grandad would have said, 'Here you are, old boy. All waiting. Haven't touched a thing.'

I used to go up there sometimes and pick out a book and look at the name on the flyleaf – Edward Beech, Oxford, 1913, 1914 – and think how it was written by a man not yet twenty, who didn't know when he wrote his name that he had only a year or two to live. Like Mum, when she left for Greece. And later when Grandad told me a bit more, I figured it all out. Edward, the second son. First Richard, then Edward. They could have afforded, in every sense, to indulge a brilliant scholar-in-the-making. Not knowing that both of them would soon be dead. One in March and one in September, 1915. It would even have looked good to have had some other-worldly and learned element in the family. So: a whole library, bought almost at one go and by the yard by a bountiful if ignorant father (Richard Beech the elder, my great-grandfather, whose strengths were ballistics and business). A whole range of classical texts in the best editions of the day, meant to last a lifetime.

And it was strange to think that if he hadn't been killed he might have been by then some distinguished Oxford professor, with a bow-tie and half-rimmed gold specs. And Grandad and I might have visited him for tea – can you imagine that, tea in a don's rooms, overlooking some ivy-encrusted court? – and I would have watched them get jealous and tetchy with each other over me.

So I became this swot. While there was rock-and-roll and Elvis and the Beatles, I became this student of the Ancients. When I wasn't riding around on Hadrian, imagining I was living in the reign of Queen Anne, I was going back a couple of thousand years more, delving into dead languages and imagining I might one day become, I don't know, something which made a virtue out of obsolescence – a curator! A brilliant female archaeologist! And all because of her, my mythical Greek mother. Until I was eighteen years old and had a place lined up at University, and I decided to do it by the direct route and go to Greece myself.

124

You think I'm just another scatty, crack-brained, washed-up Brooklyn housewife who cheats now and then on her husband? But let me tell you, I've got culture. I know about Sophocles and Plato and the Persian Wars. I used to show people around the Acropolis. No kidding. And though in the end I never took that place at University, I can still quote you, *in the original*, the first five lines of the Odyssey. Want to hear? Okay, let's skip it. And I still think that no one ever got it better, no one said it better. I mean, all that stuff – Odysseus and Penelope, Orpheus and Eurydice – it still gets to you, doesn't it? It still breaks you up.

Have you ever been to Athens? Have you ever seen the Parthenon? When you first see it, the first thing you feel is that you're amazed it's really real. Then after a while you feel sort of sorry for it, stranded up there all alone above the traffic and apartment blocks. Then if you live in Athens for any length of time, you start not to notice it, as if you're embarrassed by it, as if you'd rather pretend it's not there.

She was born in Drama. That sounds like a joke, doesn't it? Like saying: 'I grew up in Catastrophe' or 'I lived in Crisis'. But when you go to Greece all those up-in-the-air Greek words suddenly become literal and actual. Like all those names that shouldn't belong to real life. You meet a man called Adonis. And his wife Aphrodite. You go to the café Zeus.

And Drama is a town in the far north of Greece, in Macedonia, between two mountains, Mount Pangeon and Mount Falakron. And there never was a town less aptly named. Because all they do around there is watch tobacco growing, then watch it drying, then weigh it and sell it. And smoke it. While they count their money.

But drama is a funny thing, isn't it? You want it. Everyone wants it. Who doesn't want a little drama in their lives? Then when you get it, you find it's just what you can do without.

I went there, in a slow, hot, dusty train out of Salonika. And

125

I went to Thassos too (a ferry from Kavalla), where Uncle Spiro had had his village, and where I imagined him, I don't know, sitting on a balcony, reading Wordsworth and Keats, because he was a professor of English at Salonika (with a little library of English books like Uncle Edward had a library of Greek ones – I guess those two would have liked each other), and where she and he weathered out the war. But I never found the villa. Maybe it was gone anyway, or I was looking in the wrong place. And I went to Olympus. Which was easiest. Because I could pretend I was just an ordinary tourist, on an ordinary tourist coach, paying my respects to the home of the gods. And how was I to know exactly *where*? In all those mountains. I listened to the guide, babbling on about what I knew already, and I never thought that soon I would be doing a job just like hers.

I didn't find Mum. But I found out about being lonely and feeling a stranger and getting stared at. Especially about getting stared at. I know that Grandad hadn't wanted me to go. Though he'd never said. I could have spent one last, long, idle summer with him at Hyfield. I could have teased him by getting coolly and carelessly involved (I'm eighteen now, I've left school) with one of his junior execs at BMC, or – hell, why not? – with one of the married ones. Ha! Who am I kidding?

But I'd wanted to see the world. And there I was, on a Sunday afternoon in Drama, at what seemed the very edge of it. Lying on a lumpy bed in a bare hotel room overlooking a square that radiated heat and inertia, and thinking that perhaps it was just as well that Uncle Edward never got to go to Greece. Because Homer doesn't tell you about miles and miles of flat tobacco fields. Or about the sad stumps of crumbling minarets. Or that Greek men wear flat caps and have gold teeth and stubbly chins. Or they have sun-glasses and little thin moustaches. And when they are just talking normally it sounds as if they are having a fight. And the women are mostly fat and swathed in black.

I thought I would ask questions. Get to know people who'd known her. Say: I am the daughter of Anna Vouatsis. Me with my dark eyes and smattering of Greek, and a little notebook in which Grandad had written down all he could remember of what Mum had told him of before she met Harry. I thought I'd feel instant attachment to this land that was half my own. But in Drama, where on Sunday evenings the whole town suddenly swarms into the streets and starts walking up and down, just walking manically up and down and greeting one another like long-lost friends, as if to prove things are not so inert after all, I lay in that hotel room with the shutters closed, with my Blue Guide and my copy of the Odyssey, with an empty stomach and – pardon me, Doctor K – my hand between my legs. And on Thassos, when I'd given up on the villa, and when I went down in the heat of the afternoon to a little empty beach (afraid of lust-crazed youths behind every rock) and swam, it was the first time in that trip that I felt a thrill of true, truant pleasure. I might even have said aloud, with my head poking out of the water – blue sea! The sun beating off hot rocks! Think of me, Doctor K, think of my young body in that blue, clear water! – 'I'm sorry, Mum. But I came here. I'm here.'

I met him at Thermopylae. How about that? Where Leonidas held the pass, keeping the world safe for democracy. But he wasn't called Leonidas. Just Joe. And Thermopylae now is a pull-in with some road-houses where the Athens–Salonika buses take a half-hour break. On one side of the road are steep rocks and on the other is a marsh and an ugly monument to the battle.

He picked me out straight away from that busload of yawning, stretching passengers. And I had him down as English before he even spoke, because only Englishmen abroad have that faint look about them of the boy scout. Even when they're driving a white Mercedes.

You know what my first thought is? To pretend I'm Greek!

127

Defending the pass. Ha! But that lasts about two seconds. Because he says, 'You're not going all the way to Athens in that *thing*, are you?' And it's true, it was some bus. My suitcase was strapped to the roof with about a ton of other misshapen luggage, and we had a hard job persuading the driver to fetch it down.

'I'm air-conditioned,' he says. Then he laughs, the laugh of a man who wears laughter like a second skin. 'I mean, so is my car.'

He orders two beers and *souvlákia* – in a *terrible* accent – and says, What was I doing in Greece? And I say, Oh, just travelling, a tourist. You looked Greek, he says. And I say, Oh, so how did you know I wasn't? And he says, You looked lost too. And I thought, Well, okay, so that's a well-tried line: the little lost girl. So I look at him meekly and girlishly and say, 'And what are you doing in Greece?'

You see: *older men*. Schoolgirl parties. Fathers of friends. Uncle Frank even. Looking up at them all eyelashes and sweet admiration. Not even knowing I might be making them sweat. So when I meet a man, one to one, on neutral territory, in *Thermopylae* of all places, what do I do but slip into the same old role? Wanting there to be this safe buffer of an imaginary generation between us, wanting to be like a child, and wanting *him* to erase that touch of the boy scout. Which unnerves him. Because he's only twenty-five, for a start – he gets that in early. Twenty-five but a company executive. And the more he tries to play his side of it, the more he betrays that he's just a kid really, though a kid who's landed on his feet. Here he is in Greece for a whole year, working for a tour company that's just started to take off, swanning around in a hired Mercedes, doing deals and making contacts. And out of nervousness or naivety or just sheer high spirits he starts to talk to me as if I'm some client he has to impress. He says, This is the age of fun, the age of leisure, the age of the holiday – there never was a time to be alive like the 1960s.

And I'm thinking: Okay, so there's no threat here. And Jesus, *I* am the older one. My head full of Homer and Sophocles and scholarship and sage thoughts. Sophia! Sophia! You know what my name means?

So what am I doing talking to a shrink?

And I fell for him. I fell for him like I would go on falling for him, till I was pregnant. Like a mother falls for a little boy she does and doesn't want to grow up. I'd got it wrong, you see. The wrong way round. What I needed was a younger man.

We drove past signs to Chalcis and Thebes. He kept looking at me, turning his head quickly from the road as we drove. I kept my eyes ahead, but I could tell that with each glance he was a little less certain, the laughter in his face melting away. That his plan, whatever his plan had been – an old, hackneyed plan – was being modified, changed. He hadn't reckoned on *this*. He was going to have to take me seriously. And I was thinking, I shall have to tell him lots of things, the whole story of my life perhaps. Oh, and another thing I shall have to tell him: that I'm still a virgin.

I'd never felt so beautiful.

The sun was sinking. You know about the light in Greece? How it goes purple and violet and rose. Greek light. I thought: I hadn't come to Greece to find my mother. I'd come to find myself, to find my own life. And here I was, in the land of gods and heroes.

And I'd never thought the world could be so lovely. White houses stepping down to the sea on all those little islands. Painted eyes on painted boats. Olive trees turning silver in the breeze. And the lemon trees on Poros and the pines throbbing with cicadas and their own hot scent. I never thought the blue Aegean could be so blue-blue-blue. Or the days so dazzling. Or the nights so voluptuous and starlit. Or the heat so flagrant, so that you felt all the time you were really naked, just the thin sleeve of your clothes between you and the world, and you could walk down even a raucous Athens street, as brazen, as confident and erotic (oh yes, Doctor K, no longer a virgin) as those statues of striding, beaming youths in the museums.

I used to feel almost sorry sometimes for those parties I led round the Acropolis. Round Delphi and Corinth. And Mycenae and Epidauros. Because they weren't in love too? How did I know? They were on holiday, weren't they, having the time of their lives? But they could look so lost and sheepish, stumbling around those ruins, as if, without their guide, they wouldn't have known what to do. Or as if it didn't matter what the guide said or whether or not it was true, so long as she just kept talking. I used to pick out the ones who fancied me. Middle-aged husbands with straw hats and peeling noses. Not listening and not looking at what they were meant to be looking at. Nothing like knowing one man is crazy over you for spotting the others.

But when I'd finished, there would always be the ritual, the duty of the cameras. Always leave plenty of time, pause at the best places, for photographs. I used to think, Why is it so desperate, so sad, so urgent – everyone taking the same pictures? And I'd come to this conclusion: They are trying to possess something that doesn't belong to them.

I used to tell Joe sometimes – as if I were responsible: But they don't seem to *enjoy* themselves. And he'd say, 'Don't patronize the paying customer. Who knows what they feel? Maybe they've never had a holiday abroad before. Never seen the world. Eyes down all their lives. You put them suddenly in the sunshine, show them the sights. They're a little shy, a little dazzled. Like I was, goddess . . .'

That's what he used to call me. Goddess. We used to make love right there in the office on Nikodhimou. The blinds drawn and the evening noise in the street. His head in my thighs.

He said it would be easy. I knew about all that *stuff*, didn't I?

130

And I spoke some Greek. And he'd fix up my papers, no problem. Guide and courier. So I wrote to Grandad and said I wouldn't be coming home, after all, in September, in fact I wouldn't even be going to university (I'd write separately). The fact was I'd met this man, and he could get me a job. The fact was I was *happy*. And I think it was that word, heavily underlined, that made him write back, without a hint of reproach, whatever he really felt, and say I must do what I thought was best, I was eighteen now. But I would remember to write to him, wouldn't I?

So I stayed the whole winter. I stayed till Joe's year was up. I wrote Grandad letters. We had the apartment on Ippodamou Street and the place on Poros Mr Zoumboulakis lent us for weekends. They say Poros is all ruined now. In the winter there were still plenty of tour parties wanting to do Athens and trips out. Sounion. Marathon. 'Had the Athenians not won at Marathon, the whole history of our civilization might have been different.' (Got that, everyone?) In between, on the coach rides, little snippets of mythology. The deeds of Theseus. How the Aegean got its name.

Do you know what winter is like in Greece? They try to pretend it's not really happening, that there isn't really such a thing as winter. The wind blows and it rains and everyone shivers for a while. Then the sky clears and goes still and blue. Out come the café tables again. People sit and chatter, their breath steaming. On the trees that line the streets there are little bright balls like miniature suns. Oranges.

I won't forget that April morning when I looked out of the window on Ippodamou Street and saw the tank in the square below. It was like when I first saw the Parthenon, all floodlit, that night we drove into Athens. I thought: This isn't really real, this isn't a real tank. It looked like some clumsy, extinct monster that has somehow turned up in the wrong place and was trying to get out.

131

The streets were all empty.

You know, Joe went back there in '74. To 'clear some things up'. That was the summer Argosy Tours folded. But I didn't think he had anything more to do with them. And I don't know how he *knew*. I mean, about Cyprus and everything. He said it was strange, the whole country was mobilizing, and yet the tourists were still carrying on as normal, buying postcards and getting their sun-tans. He said that almost straight away they started pulling down all those phoenix-and-soldier signs that were the emblem of the Junta. He said he never thought you could feel, see a thrill run through a whole people like that. I had this picture of a breeze running through a field. He was gone three weeks. When he got back he looked so tired. The tired old new world. That's when I fucked Nick the plumber. We all want Greece in our hearts, don't we? Blue air and marble Apollos.

HARRY

To be happy in Nuremberg! To fall in love in Nuremberg! In that city of guilt and grief and retribution, to think of only one face, one pair of eyes, one body.

Sometimes I wonder, if it had been somewhere else, if it would have happened so quickly, so precipitately. As if there you could do these things, dispense with niceties and preliminaries. Like the German girls, whose English was basic: 'Kommon, shveetart, less go ficken.' If we would have walked as we walked that afternoon across the Hauptmarkt, trembling just a little (though the autumn air was mild), with nothing between us save a few words, a few cups of so-called coffee and a mutual rush of desire. (We stopped outside the Frauenkirche: she lifted her head and took those deep, concentrated breaths.) If she would have led me so directly and so artlessly to where she stayed, Küfergasse, number twenty-eight, and I would have heard so soon, like the unfamiliar sound of happiness, like the sound of the future being unveiled without any pious ceremony, the slither of a dress being lifted over newly bought American nylons.

A virgin, for all that. A towel to protect her landlady's sheets. Why then? Why me? As if she were shutting other, bigger doors than the door of that little dingy room in Nuremberg, behind her.

There was a look you could see in those days in people's faces. Maybe you could see it especially in Nuremberg. As if their minds had gone on hurriedly ahead, grown up too fast, and their bodies had been left behind. They were waiting for their bodies to catch up with their minds. Or for their minds to go back to their innocent, forgotten bodies.

Küfergasse, *achtundzwanzig*. I still remember the names of the streets. Burgstrasse, Tetzelgasse, Küfergasse. An archway, two flights of stairs. The room with the yellowed wallpaper and the paler rectangles left by removed pictures (the Führer? Frames for firewood?), where we told each other the story of our lives.

Tobacco. They were all in tobacco. Save the only one who was left now, Uncle Spiro, the scholar, who years ago had packed his bags and gone to study in Athens and, later, England. When she was twelve years old her mother and father had died, vainly trying to beat out the flames that were consuming their tobacco warehouse. Then her two brothers were killed in the early months of the war, and she had passed into the care of her uncle, by now a professional academic and a widower. To avoid starvation, or worse, he had abandoned his apartment in Salonika and they had gone to live during the occupation in his summer house on the island of Thassos.

I said (but this was like a made-up story, a hastily improvised bedtime story, to stop her tears): There was this son who didn't get on with his father. And this old house in leafy Surrey, with a gravel drive and lawns and an orchard. And wasn't it funny, but I had had an uncle once who was a scholar too. Of Greek. But he had never (so far as I knew) gone to bed with a Greek woman.

(He had never, so far as I knew, gone to bed with any woman.)

134

She said, drying her eyes: Was it true that in England everyone took tea at precisely four o'clock? And ate cucumber sandwiches?

The lights from the traffic in Tetzelgasse used to flicker across the ceiling. I still see it. A small sliver appearing in one corner, then quickening, widening. The exact pattern of those cracks in the ceiling.

But had he really sworn never to see me again? And what did he do, to have this big house?

Not so big, I said. I said: He made something. I didn't want to tell her. I said: Guess. It was like tobacco. It went up in smoke too.

I was a photographer, there to capture on film the face of evil. She was a translator, there to translate and transcribe the evidence of killings, atrocities, burnings, little white Greek villages razed to the ground.

To be happy in Nuremberg. To smile in Nuremberg. To get up and get dressed and go out into the Nuremberg night like a young couple from the country, snatching a few stolen days in some pleasure-loving city.

The photo, not the photographer? Only the picture counts? Does it matter, when the photographer lifts the camera to capture the face of evil, if a voice is chuckling inside him: 'I am happy, I am in love'?

We were married by an army chaplain on October 14th, 1946, two weeks after the Tribunal passed sentence. She wrote to her uncle. He would give his blessing, no question. (A real Englishman!) After that, she was always 'going' to see him – when the fighting was over in Greece, when he was settled again in Salonika, when Sophie was a bit older.

I wired to my paper – impudently, since I had only been employed by them for six months – to request a week's 'matrimonial leave'. We had little money, but I used my press credentials to 'borrow' a car and a spare jerrycan of petrol, and

135

we drove, through Ulm and round Lake Constance, to Switzerland, feeling as we explained ourselves to the guards at the border, like escapees. To neutral Switzerland, where the white peaks under fresh autumn snow really did seem like the icing on some gigantic, never-to-be-eaten cake, and the wooden chalets nestling on the slopes really did seem like life-size musical boxes that had dropped from the sky. And Herr and Frau Hebinger, stolid proprietors of the Pension Hirsch near Lucerne, who gave the impression that they truly didn't know, cut off behind that veil of mountains, what had been going on in the world, and who believed that Anna, the first Greek in their guest-book, must be, in these northern climes, continually cold, became almost fond, almost paternal, their dour faces cracked, when I explained that the last thing, the very last thing my new wife was, was cold.

To dance in Nuremberg! The 'Arkadien' (who gave it that name?) in Lorenzerstrasse. A pianist, a drummer, a guitarist, a trombonist. And the people getting up to recover their lost bodies on the little dance floor. I should have photographed those faces in the 'Arkadien', veiled in smoke and uncertainty. The faces that said, Is it all right now, will it ever be all right, to lead lives of our own?

I should have photographed that couple – and called it for ever afterwards (the blasphemy!) 'Nuremberg, 1946'. That ecstatic couple, glimpsed (so how *could* I have photographed them?) in the gilt-framed mirror – miracle of preservation – above the bar.

Your mother and father, Sophie. Anna and me, dancing in Nuremberg.

SOPHIE

———

Dear Paul, dear Tim. You were there at the time, at the very
scene. But you never saw, you never knew a thing. When I lay
in that hospital all those terrible hours, that thought suddenly
occurred to me and I clung to it for safety. You were there but
so perfectly ignorant. I was like a black cloak around you; you
were like a little warm light.

And that was the first time I felt that you actually existed,
that this wasn't just some condition of *mine*: 'being pregnant'.
(Except that I was ignorant too, wasn't I? Because I never
imagined – twins!) And when Joe came and sat by my bed that
afternoon and I said to him, It's all right – I mean, *that*'s all
right, I haven't miscarried or anything – I knew in a flash (ha!
– a flash!) that my whole allegiance had changed. He held my
hand and looked at me intently, but he didn't know where I
was. I was in another room. He was like a man who'd opened
the wrong door and seen something terrible. But it was okay
because you could step out quickly. Quick! Shut the door!
Quick! Now he was back, or so he thought, where he belonged.
If you just kept to your place the world would fall back together
again. But I was still inside that room. I always would be. The
only thing was, *you* would be there with me. And that wishful,

wilful innocence of his, it wasn't a patch on yours, which was the real, pure thing.

You see, my darlings, the way it's been? Oh yes, I guessed that from early on he knew that I needed you more than I needed him. Saw that; made that sacrifice, and never raised a begrudging murmur. Not that he doesn't need you too. Maybe you've already figured out how those evening fool-arounds in the backyard aren't just for pure fun. He's saying: Let me have my turn. Maybe you've even worked out – or one day you will – that almost without knowing it, he's starting to put in bigger claims. You'll be grown-up soon, after all, real young lads. Using the one damn fact – you're his own sex! – that works to his advantage. So what's the harm anyway in kids playing with toy guns?

Maybe he's got it taped. Just wait. They'll react, shake off their clinging mother and turn out to be Daddy's boys through and through. And it'll be all my own dumb fault.

Except that I know he doesn't think that far, or that sharp. He's made the concession. For my sake. Give her time. Bow to circumstances; accept it. Ten years of allowances. I could weep for him sometimes. Though I stopped loving him long ago. That's the honest truth, my darlings. I think I stopped loving him that time he came and held my hand in the hospital. I think I stopped loving anyone then. Except you.

But I know that he still loves me. As much as he ever did. Loves me so much that he'd never guess, never imagine – How to smash someone's world, my pets. He looks at me sometimes like a guilty character in a comedy, peering wistfully at a character in a tragedy. Still calls me 'Goddess'. But don't get ideas, Joe, there's nothing noble or sublime about me. And I'd stick to comedy if I were you. It's more fun. He looks at me as if he's actually glad, like some willing penitent, to have this chance, this ten-year-long chance, to express his love by looking after me, by being truly considerate towards me.

It's just that he doesn't fuck me any more. Or he fucks me

138

gently, reverently, as if he's fucking some fragile, precious china doll. As if he's had this notion that I had this nasty shock which changed me back into an innocent little kid. Not a lady you can fuck.

But I'm not a little kid.

(Am I, Doctor K?)

The facts of life, my darlings. Your parents fuck. They don't fuck. Your Mummy fucks around. Your Dad is good about things. Because he's good, she fucks. Gets fucked. Is all fucked-up.

Once upon a time, my angels, there used to be this ritual when parents would take their children aside and tell them the facts of life. But nowadays it doesn't happen so much. It's not so necessary, because in this well-informed and hyper-communicative world, the facts of life float freely in the air (what do you hear when you walk down the street? – fuckfuckfuck). They just seep in.

I never went through this ritual. Because my mother – And my father – And I think Grandad gave up on the facts of life when he gave up his right arm. I learnt the facts of life from schoolfriends, and from guesswork. And then again from Joe. But even then I never learnt them properly.

Ha! If only the facts of life were like they sound. So essential, so vital, so all-inclusive. As if they were truly all you need to know. But there are other facts of life, besides those much-broadcast ones, my darlings, that your mother has to tell you.

So are you listening? Are you ready . . . ?

You were there at the funeral, but you never knew it. Though without you your mother would never have got through that terrible day. Or those terrible weeks and months. You were there when I said goodbye for the last time to your grandfather, though you never saw him. You were inside your mother's tummy (fact of life number one: all children come from their mother's tummy). But your mother was inside her tummy with

139

you, imagining a world where you didn't have to see or know. And if you're smart and clued-up, the way kids are these days, you'll say: Sure, we figured all that – but where were we, where did we come from before we were inside your tummy? That's what your mother is trying to explain.

You have never seen your grandfather and he has never seen you. Though you have heard me mention from time to time this far-away person, like some character in a story-book, called Harry. But that's how he always was for me too, a far-away person. Which is strange, because I think now that what he might say, in his own defence, is that he tried to get close to certain things. The things that most people don't want to get close to. Once upon a time, or so people say, he was a distinguished man, a photographer.

You have never seen England, though that's where your mother and father are from. But you have seen enough pictures of it in the brochures Joe brings home from work, which makes it look like some high-class Disneyland. And Joe has said from time to time, One day we will all go to England. And I've said, Yes. But not yet.

You never saw your great-grandfather, though you were there at the graveside when they buried what was left of him. He was a hero, you see. A real hero. His business was in – But that's another story.

I haven't seen Harry since that time I said goodbye to him ten years ago. And he hasn't seen me. Out of sight, out of – But Doctor Klein (who you've never seen either) says that's the oldest lie in the world. Come here, my darlings. Come close to your mother. He tried to get close to certain things. Certain facts of life. It's just that he wasn't much good at closeness. And I wouldn't have to tell you these things. Why should I ever have to tell you these things? I really meant it, you see: Goodbye for ever. But now he writes me this letter, my angels, and in the letter he says –

HARRY

She makes me feel – hell, she makes me feel that I'm half my age, that everything is possible. She makes me sing, unapologetically (Michael and Peter give me tolerant looks) above the noise of the Cessna while we hang like a lark over Wiltshire, waiting for the dormant Bronze Age to emerge with the green flush of spring. She makes me feel that the world is never so black with memories, so grey with age, that it cannot be re-coloured with the magic paint-box of the heart.

In Switzerland, by the shores of Lake Lucerne (ducks scooting and clucking in the thin sunshine), I told Anna about Dad, spinning this tale of a life-long enemy, an implacable ogre who would bar the door against me should I so much as dare to seek shelter, with my new wife, under his roof again. I should have predicted – I should have learnt by then – that it would be otherwise. That when I summoned up the nerve to break the news and even to propose a visit, I would suddenly become the Prodigal Son, while to Anna he would be the model father-in-law.

I still see them, walking in the orchard. Him talking, her listening. November leaves on the grass. I had slipped in to fetch Anna's scarf. But I stood for a while at the window, twisting the scarf in my hands, and twisting something else inside me. I didn't feel angry, not even wrong-footed. I didn't feel I should have to protest to Anna: But this is all an act, you wait and see. I didn't answer the voice that was whispering in my head: You see what he is doing, you see what the old bastard's doing – he's going to try to bring you round through her, he's going to hope that now you will change your mind. (I even thought: And suppose – ? And supposing – ?)

That afternoon – after suffering all morning the worst anticipations – Anna had given me the first, fleeting glance she had ever given me of distrust. As if she had said: Do we share the same reality, you and I? But then her glance had flickered on, in happy credulity, to take in the weathered brick and old oak of Hyfield. And I didn't feel a sting (I could bridge that gap of suspicion) at that look of reproach.

They paused under one of the apple trees. He was extolling, perhaps, like some benign old landowner, the virtues of the English pippin. Be careful, Anna. Just remember what really grows in that orchard. A moment when she laughed – laughter at Hyfield! – and the chime of her laughter, and the clatter of his, reached the house in the damp, melancholy air.

Hyfield. Autumn in England. A smoky stillness. A settled-ness.

And why didn't I feel all those things? Why did I stand at that window, unwilling to break the glass of that little vision, the spell of that little scene. Because I could see – it wasn't an act – that he was captivated.

A lover's pride. But more than that.

They turned to walk slowly back towards the house. (Should I go out now – interrupt? – with the scarf?) The familiar, limp hang of his right arm seemed at that moment to accentuate rather than detract from the life in the rest of his body. What shall I say – he looked young? As if, right then, it wasn't Anna

142

I loved, so much as him. As if for me too that picture I had drawn for Anna of my father, along with all the grievance and hate that had been etched into it, were an illusion.

SOPHIE

And you see, Doctor K, I don't want to screw up that letter and throw it away. (Though I've hidden it from Joe.) And I don't want to say: And screw you too, Harry, for an old fornicator. I don't even feel – do you know what I mean? – cheated. Jilted. The truth is I want it to be wonderful. Wonderful. I want to go. Can you believe that? I want to write back to him and say, Yes, yes, I'm coming. I'm coming, for your wedding. I want to pack a suitcase and bundle the twins into a cab to JFK and tell them on the journey all about that little old country where I was born. I want him, and her, whoever she is (but I hope she's as lovely as a princess), to be waiting at the airport. I want to throw my arms around him and feel his arms round mine. Harry Dad Father. Your grandchildren. And I want to hug her too and kiss her like a sister, a younger sister, and say, I hope you'll be happy with him, because I never was. Shit, I know this is pure theatre, I know this is like a bad movie, like the way it isn't. But what's the point of life, and what's the point of goddam movies, if now and then you can't discover that the way you thought it isn't, the way you thought it only ever is in movies, really is the way it is?

JOE

—

Well, if you ask me, I know there was never any big thing going for me, no plan, no special assignments. I was what you call an 'accident', or an almost-accident. A visitor, that's all. An extra guest at the party.

And the truth is I'm happy when other people are happy round me. I'm glad when other people are happy. And there are plenty of people who can't give that for an excuse.

People say to me, people I know and meet at work, 'Hey, Joe, you know, you're an easy-going kind of guy. Always good to be with. What's the secret?' And I say any number of things. Like: 'It's policy.' Or: 'It's the new after-shave.' Or: 'It's the influence of this fair city of yours, and your fresh American way.' Or I want to say, But it's the other way round: I'm looking at someone who's smiling at *me*, and the reason why I'm smiling is because smiles are infectious. But the fact is I really don't have an answer.

People like to be with me. They like to be with me! And I never knew how to explain it or exploit it. And maybe if I could do either, they wouldn't like to be with me. Mr Nice. Mr No Threat. Mr No Complications. People like a regular dummy. One of the girls we once had here once said to me: 'Mr Carmichael, you're kinda *good company* – you could take advantage of that.' Crossing her legs and biting her pen. And I said: 'But that might spoil all the innocent fun we're going to have.' When she left about a year later there was a little packet from her sneaked into my in-tray. A pair of pink panties appliquéd 'Love from Arlene', and a message: 'Now you can't say you never got them off me. Thanks for the innocent fun.'

But that was years ago (I put them in my desk drawer: what do you do with a pair of panties especially inscribed to you?), before Sophie got like she wasn't interested any more. Nowadays, maybe . . .

And, come to think of it, it's been a long time since anyone at the office has said to me, 'Hey, Joe, you're fun to be with.'

A couple of months ago Gary and Jack and Karen made a point of keeping me at Mario's, the beers coming one after the other. I could see what the plan was. They were thinking: Our Mr C's actually starting to look a little distant, to lose his smile. They were thinking maybe they could get me to talk, just a little. About Sophie. Maybe they could ask. But before we could get that far, I put down my beer and looked at them all, and just said, 'You're good people.' There was this pause and they lowered their eyes. Then I told a joke about Reagan and zero options. Then we had a fun evening anyway. I called Sophie and got home half drunk. She didn't mind. I wish she had.

She used to drop by, of course, once. Sometimes with the boys. When she went on shopping sprees. She used to try and embarrass me by doing this imitation, in front of everybody, of the spendthrift wife, taking things out of bags from Macy's and Gimbels. And I used to go through this act of madly feeling my pockets, as if I couldn't find my wallet or my charge cards. No one was to know she has her own income from the money her Grandad left her. We're still cushioned by that money: what she started to call some while back her 'stock-pile'. But I wouldn't have cared anyway. I'd have let her burn hundreds, thousands. When she came in like that, all mischievous and breathless, and only a little too shrill, I used to think: It's all right. It'll be all right.

I go to Mario's most evenings. Sometimes with some of the others, sometimes alone. More often alone these days. Just for a beer before I head home. Mario pours the beer without my asking, brings over the dish of pretzels, and always comes out with a line. 'Mr Carmichael, I see you're offering tours to the Falkland Islands now.' 'Yes, Mario, you want the *Canberra* or the *QE2*?' Always 'Mr Carmichael'. He loves it. So English upper class. And that accent! (My accent, Mario, what part of it hasn't turned American, is North London: Tottenham. That's a cheap accent.)

If I sit in Mario's and there's a group near me at a table or the bar, and they're laughing, their talk is warm and flowing, that makes me feel good too. True. It's enough isn't it? Voices. Laughter. The chink of glasses, smell of food. The cars and people passing on 38th. Sometimes it reminds me of Greece. That's what I loved about it out there. The life on the streets. The brightness and colour and chatter of it all. It's true, I never cared much about ruins and temples and statues. Or even cypress trees and olive groves. Until I met Sophie I was always embarrassed by the word 'beautiful'. She taught me about all that. The twelve gods of Olympus, the nine muses. Let me see now, Mario, if I can remember the nine muses . . .

I'm a surface person. I like it to sparkle and ripple. 'Buoyant' is the word they use. I float easy. And you can go on floating even when you're way out of your depth.

I used to love it when I first started coming here. On hot evenings. With my tie loosened and my copy of the *Post*. Just like a real New Yorker. Give me the settings, give me the props. Joe Chameleon, that's me. Spelt: Carmichael. Joseph of the rainbow-coloured coat. I think I could have been an actor once. Easy. When I was a kid in the boy scouts, we did this

149

Christmas Show, in the Church Hall, Stapleton Road. Our troop and another. There was this spot where I had to step out to the front and do this monologue (written by the assistant scout-master). Real corny jokes. I thought: I won't make it. They'll stare right through me. They'll think: This kid's a flop. But I was a hit. They laughed. I loved it. Even added a line or two of my own. I can still see those laughing faces behind the dazzle of the lights. I'm making them laugh! Me! And I can still hear the scout-master saying to my parents, 'It seems young Joe has quite a talent for the stage.' And Dad saying, 'My son's name is Joseph.'

It's changed, Mario. It's changing. Is this how it is for everybody? I used to think that happiness was *out there*. All around. All I had to do was get to it. Now – I know, I can feel it – I'm becoming this sort of sentry on duty. Like happiness is *inside*, hidden away, and I'm trying to keep out all the bad things. Those letters I write to Harry. Like a loyal, clandestine son-in-law. Sophie's fine. She's fine. Meaning: Stay out of it, Harry. She's safe with me. I know what you thought of me. I know the only person you wanted to marry Sophie was someone just like yourself. But she belongs to me now.

She's not fine. Not fine at all.

Jesus, Mario, I wanted to see the world, but there was always part of me that wanted to be this cliché, this jerk: this guy who gets out his wallet with the photos of his smiling wife and smiling kids, and says: There, that's my ticket! That's my little stake in humanity, my little bundle of joy!

Make her safe, make her happy again. Please, Doctor Klein.

'Hey, but those are two big guys, Mr Carmichael. Now, don't tell me, this is Paul and this is Tim. No? I got it wrong again?'

Nearly ten years now, but when I look out of my office window I still get that feeling I got when we first came here. New York! Wow! Is this real? It's just like in all those films. But now I'm going to step through the screen.

150

The strange thing is, after all this time, I still haven't stepped through the screen. There's still this – gap. But maybe that's how I like it now. A dream city. Step through the screen and you lose the picture.

When I was twelve years old, in '53, my parents bought a television so we could watch the Coronation of Queen Elizabeth. I never understood this, since, living in Tottenham, there was nothing to stop us catching a bus to Westminster and watching the real thing. But I think I knew even then that the real reason for getting that TV was to fill the gap between them and me. Even today, Mario, I can't look at a TV without feeling a twinge of rivalry. You know, like the TV was a favoured brother. Like it was this perfectly charming, perfectly obliging lodger. But I have to be thankful too. Because to me it was also like a little chink in the cell wall, showing me what lay beyond. And if to them the pictures were just pictures – it didn't matter what they were, so long as they kept coming, filling the vacuum of our living-room – I knew that one day I would show them you could make the pictures real.

If they could see me now. In New York! In America! If they could have seen me in Greece. Driving a white Merc by the blue Med! If they could have seen my wedding. Hyfield. Chauffeurs! Silverware! Champagne!

I was even on TV myself once, wasn't I? Sophie Carmichael, with her husband, leaving Dorking General Hospital . . . Though I wasn't in a position – in fact it was terrible, bloody terrible, being the wrong side of the screen – to wave. Hi Mum! Hi Dad! This is me!

Remember me?

What the TV said was that a good time was coming. There was our new Queen, in a gilt coach, riding to be crowned. And there was Edmund Hillary and Sherpa Tensing looking like spacemen, standing on the top of the world with a Union Jack stuck between them. What the TV said was that there were

151

people who weren't like Mum and Dad. That you could tune in and latch on to things the way I latched on to Terry Gray. His sister was the second big love of my life. (Who was the first? You want to know, Mario? Queen Elizabeth, of course. Black and white and blurred though she was.) Not that I got anywhere with Gillian Gray. Never even ruffled her six – or was it eight? Or twelve? – stiff petticoats. But this chaste and honourable behaviour put me in with her brother. And Terry Gray's father ran this tidy little business called Riviera Travel. And Gillian Gray had friends.

Dad said the Army would beat it out of me. The Army would teach me a thing or two. And so it did. It taught me to drive. And it taught me to wait. And even month after month at Catterick Camp was preferable to being eighteen and still living with Mum and Dad at number thirty, Davenport Road. When Terry and I were both back in civvy street we celebrated, on his father's money and his father's business card, by motoring to the South of France in an Austin Healey 3000. Paris! Nice! Monte Carlo! *Bonjour Mesdemoiselles! Mais oui! C'est bon! Voulez-vous coucher avec moi?* But by then it was all starting to happen with a Whoosh. Right through to the magic mid-Sixties. By which time there was money and clothes and sex and travel and being English suddenly meant you were swinging, and I was old enough not just to be enjoying it all but to be making a fair whack out of it and helping it along, a canny step or two ahead of the tide, in the direction of sunny Spain, Italy and Greece.

Argosy Tours. The new child of Riviera Travel, about to swallow its parent. Terry divided the map like a general. I got sent to Greece.

You know, Mario, I still find it hard to say the word 'vacation'. 'Holiday' sounds to me like fun. 'Vacation' sounds like a bowel movement. If you say the word 'holiday', what I still see is a table. Some wine. Raffia-backed chairs. A table outside, under an awning or a sun umbrella, or just under the warm stars, in some place where there are palm trees and cicadas and vines, things that will always seem exotic to someone born in England.

And yet for ten years now I have been busily sending people to the country I once so wanted to leave. Where it can rain all summer and where they have never discovered the café. But people want to go there. Americans above all. They have dreams of sweet old England. Oh yes, I don't deny it, I sell dreams.

But I still think that it's a good business, a happy business. It ought to work that way, oughtn't it? The trade rubbing off on the trader. No dirt, just people's holidays. We watch them come through the doors and we show them the pictures. And then we send them off, through the screen, and who knows if the pictures aren't going to come real?

'Why, Mr Carmichael, working in this office is almost like a vacation in itself.'

As if I could have taken that job Frank Irving offered me.

But here's a picture for you, Mario. Another photo from the wallet. Mum and Dad. Margate, Kent. August '61. A beach photographer must have ambushed them, because I wasn't there at the time. I was in the South of France. You can tell they're on holiday by the way they're gritting their teeth. No, they don't exactly look like a load of laughs. But then, you wouldn't believe that within two years of that photo they would both be dead. Shall I tell you the sad story of those two strangers, my parents?

They were so far away from me. You could have fitted a whole generation between them and me. She was almost forty when they married, and he was forty-two, and they must never have expected to produce me. Two last-chancers, signing on with each other. He was a big man, as you can see, but with a weak chest since childhood and a dry, grating cough that always used to proclaim: This is my cough, this is my affliction. But I

153

don't complain, no, I never complain, because, though life is no picnic, I have A Secure Job and I will one day reap the reward of A Good Pension.

She was like a parrot sitting on his shoulder. A dull, cabbage-coloured parrot. What he said, she said. Except that now, when I think of how quickly he went downhill after she died, it seems it was really she who kept him together.

They – we – used to go every year to Margate. Always Margate. Always the first two weeks in August. And always the Thanet Hotel, which was a posh name for a seaside boarding house run by a Mrs Goff, who would have had no trouble running Catterick barracks.

In the photo it's their last holiday together, though not in the sense either of them would have imagined. The next year was going to be their last holiday, because after that there was only the Big Holiday. Retirement. He'd be sixty-five. But a week before that last holiday, in July '62, she died. Collapsed in the grocer's in Bruce Grove. Hospital. Dead. What – or who – you never really knew, you never really miss, do you? I had to phone Mrs Goff to cancel for him, because he was terrified of 'letting her down'. Please don't be angry with me, Mrs Goff, but you see, unfortunately, my wife has died. But the following summer, as the first independent act of his fully pensioned status, he was there again, all by himself. First two weeks in August. And that really was the last holiday, because, come Christmas, he was in St George's Hospital near Epping, all tucked away in its own discreet and leafy grounds.

Margate! The Thanet Hotel! Jugs of tea for the beach! I suppose I should remember happy days, making sandcastles, the sun on my back. But what I remember most about Margate is the smell of tar. Sticky tar and seaweed. The suspicious trickles that ran across the beach out of holes beneath the promenade. Brown rust streaks on the concrete and rust clogging the struts under the pier, which always reminded me of shit. As if there were some unwritten English law that pleasure couldn't be pleasure without a good tang of disgust. I used to say to him: Go somewhere else, do something different. Go *abroad*. For Christ's sake, get it into your thick skull, I'm loaded, I'm offering. I'll arrange it all. But I'd see his big frame starting to judder and I'd back off fast. And when I said, 'abroad', he'd give me this boggle-eyed, disbelieving stare, as if I'd said, 'Moon'.

The polite phrase used to be 'in an institution'. But he was always in an institution. The institution of virtuous drudgery. The institution of married life, the institution of the Thanet Hotel. The institution of his own prehistoric upbringing – it was when we were getting ready for that televised Coronation, setting up the aerial and adjusting the curtains, that he announced with a voice like a knell, just in case we should get too festive and too carried away by these modern inventions, that he could remember the funeral of Queen Victoria. Think of that, Mario! He could remember the funeral of Queen Victoria. He couldn't *not* be in an institution. And the worst of those few visits I made before he died, to St George's Hospital, Epping, was that he never said : I want to get out of here.

Because I sure as hell did. After only five minutes. Quick! Out! Fresh air, normality! Quick! Quick! Thank God he went so soon. Thank God his lungs beat his mind to it, by a long chalk. Because I couldn't have gone on going to see him in that place. Those corridors! That smell. Like some evil intensification of the smell of Mrs Goff's hallway. I couldn't have borne watching him become like some of those *things* in there.

There was this grand entrance hall, which utterly belied what you were going to see inside, with a marble plaque telling you that the place had been built – in eighteen sixty-something – to house orphans. Of the *Crimean War*! And above the plaque was this huge picture, which wouldn't let you go by without looking at it, of St George and the Dragon. That was

155

the first time it ever struck me, Mario: the patron saint of my country wasn't a saint like you think of a saint – you know, holy, gentle, *saintly*. He was this chain-mailed thug, jamming a spear down the throat of a writhing beast. And dragons never existed, did they? They're supposed to be mythical, aren't they? But in this picture the dragon was much more *alive*, much more realistically painted than St George. It must have scared the pants off all those little orphans.

And now I was an orphan too . . .

Some unthinkable night in the Blitz? Some topsy-turvy moment in the Anderson shelter when the bombs were getting close and the lamp blew out and they thought, if not now, then maybe never? I was a war baby. June 1941. I don't remember any of it, of course. But I have to thank Hitler and Goering and the poor aim of the Luftwaffe for the bomb-site in Thorndyke Road, three blocks from Davenport Road, which gave me somewhere to play when I was young, out of the shadow of home. Kids' games. Cowboys and Indians. Cops and Robbers. English and Jerries, naturally. Bang bang! You're dead! What do you think, Mario, is it wrong? Is it wrong for kids to play that sort of game?

Dad thought it was wrong, of course. 'Running the streets'. It's not the streets, Dad, it's a bomb-site. But I reckoned it was worth it. He tried to wop me once for hanging out down there. I saw his arm go back, but Mum stopped him. Not that she was taking my side. She just said calmly, 'No need for that, Eric.' And he stopped dead.

It was all brambles and nettles down there where the houses had been, and garden shrubs run wild. Like a little nature reserve. One warm Sunday morning there was this lizard just sitting on an old lump of masonry, right in front of my nose. Who'd expect to see a lizard in Tottenham? I remember looking at it, and then making a grab for it. And then the lizard was gone but I was holding its tail between my fingers, and I thought, Oh God, what have I done? I've ripped a lizard in half, for no reason at all. But there wasn't any mess, just this dry bit of tail. And when I asked my teacher, she said they could do that, just shed their tails, then grow another one. And then I thought, It's okay. He'll be all right. And so will I.

That's one of the first things I noticed when Terry Gray and I went to the South of France. And again in Greece. Lizards. See them everywhere. Big ones, small ones. Green, black. On the slopes of the Acropolis. On Poros, in the garden of the villa. On the white-washed stones. Even inside, clinging to the walls. Maybe dragons are just big lizards. I told Sophie once about my London lizard. I said if I wasn't human, that's what I'd be. On a warm stone, lapping up the sun. Something bad comes along, like St George in his chain-mail, you just dart away. All you lose is the skin of your arse.

Something bad.

Sophie, come here. I want to lick the salt off you. Off every bit of you. Perfect skin on your arse, and all over. Greek skin. Made for sunshine. Sophie, you know what I like about this country? It feels like it's a holiday all the time . . .

Zoumboulakis liked to talk business in his car. He'd take me to the Plaka. Or to Tourkolimani or Vougliameni. We'd eat platefuls of seafood, watch the yachts and the half-dressed girls. Then we'd get into his big, cool Lincoln and he'd snap his fingers to the driver to just cruise around.

'Mr Carmichael, how wise of you – how wise of your company – to give you the opportunity to come and see for yourself. The good merchant always samples his own wares. And you are becoming, I think, just a little bit Greek?'

We would take one of the coast roads or just circle the city. Along Venizelou, Patission and Alexandras, then back along King Constantine, past the Zappeion and the Acropolis.

He would get out his cigarettes. Silver case. Offer me one.

Then that incongruous, ethnic-looking cigarette-holder. Carved yellow wood. His face never lost its look of glee.

'Mr Carmichael, I have a friend. A ship-owner. Yes, I know, every Greek will tell you that. But in this case both things are true – the ship-owner and the friendship. My friend not only owns ships, but, like every good ship-owner, he owns land. Lots of land. Land – as you say – 'ripe for development'. He wishes to take advantage of this 'tourist boom' we have discussed so much. He wishes to build hotels – 'international' hotels and villas. But he needs – backers.'

'He's a ship-owner and he needs backers?'

'Even ship-owners do not have everything. Let us say, though, it is a matter of friends in the right places. Not friends, you understand, like me – humble and ineffective. He has friends but they are not yet in a position to help him. He will help them, they will help him. Meanwhile, he has enemies. You understand? It is a matter also of timing. But then again it is a matter of personality. My friend is timid. Powerful but timid. For the same reason that he must wait for his friends to help him, he fears that this tourist boom we are all expecting may be – 'nipped in the bud'. How can this be, eh Mr Carmichael? My country is poor, but we have our sunshine. Who can take that from us? But my friend is timid – a fact of advantage, I need not tell you, to those who do business with him. He needs backers for his backers. But let me explain to you this mystery . . .'

When I rode round with Zoumboulakis like that I used to think, Is this really happening? Is this really me, Joe Carmichael? Driving around Athens, under the palm trees, past the white buildings, doing business with the friends of ship-owners? Any moment now I will be flicked back to Davenport Road and discover that it's all only something on the television. All only a dream.

But I have this formula with dreams, Mario. Never pinch

yourself to check. If it's good, why not take the trip? If it's bad, why discover that you can no longer tell yourself: But it's only a dream?

How much did I really know and how much did I pretend to myself that I didn't? And how much, anyway, did I *believe*? That agreement I signed with Zoumboulakis was so wrapped in conditions, so all in the future, that I thought it would never take effect. And yet the bonanza of discounts and concessions it offered to Argosy Tours was too good not to hold on option. And, besides, this wasn't my country and my business was just tourism. And I was high – just floating – on sunshine and freedom. And love.

'Joe, you make me laugh, Joe. Joe, you're good to be with.'

The last time he picked me up in that Lincoln was just a week after the coup. A brilliant day in late April, one of those warm, rich spring days with a southerly breeze, when it already seems like full summer. So that you felt it was all only some strange diversion – nothing essential had changed. The schools and public buildings were open again, and either because of this or because of the curfew at night or simply because of the weather, the streets seemed more crowded than ever. The cafés were full, the kiosks were as stacked as ever with foreign magazines, and, as Zoumboulakis himself pointed out, there was no short-age of coach parties, winding their way up to the Parthenon.

He said Karatsivas (we were naming names now) was having a little midday reception and it was time that we met.

He was different that day. More playful and familiar. As if, before, he had aped a certain English composure, but now he could show his true, loosened-up Greek self. When we drew up outside that huge place in Kifissiá, he buttoned his jacket and visibly stiffened, but with a hint of mischief, as if we were two boys on our first day in a new school. And, strangely enough, for this I actually felt fond of him for the first time.

I don't remember Karatsivas clearly. I recall a man with a

high, domed forehead, grey sideburns and a cosmopolitan, faintly vexed manner. 'Ah, Mr Carmichael. But you are so young! Our mutual venture has been blessed, so it seems. Your health, Mr Carmichael. To success. You can rely at all times, I assure you, on Mr Zoumboulakis.' And that was all. He turned to another guest. I was even glad to feel like a minor item on his agenda.

I don't recall Karatsivas clearly, because though it was his party and his house, it seemed he was not quite at the centre of it, it was not quite what he would have planned. And what I do remember about that party is the soldiers. The soldiers at the front gates, the parked jeeps, the soldiers visible across the lawns, under the pines and eucalyptus beyond the wire fence, standing on guard with white helmets and rifles. And the soldiers, officers, in peaked caps and sharply pressed uniforms, who seemed to make up the majority of the guests – none of them high-ranking or dripping with braid, but all of them wearing an expression of saintly authority.

Zoumboulakis steered me back to the car. He was drunk, but my head seemed stubbornly clear. 'Now, Mr Joseph, now we have done our duty and paid our respects – to lunch! You are hungry? Vougliameni, I think? On a day like today.'

We avoided the city centre and took the country road. A long drive to the east. I didn't speak and he seemed prepared for this. He loosened his tie, gave a belch or two and turned his head to the window, tapping his knee and hissing a tune through his teeth. On the road out of Halandri we passed whole rows of stationary armoured cars, dusty from recent manoeuvres. Then as we drove along the green slopes of Hymettos, he started to rapturize about spring in Attica.

'But your English spring is something too. You know, I was in your country for two years, in the war. In Chatham. I have seen your "Garden of England". Your "toast-houses".'

He was waiting for me to pass comment, and like a true

Englishman I had buttoned my lip. It was only as we came down into Vougliameni itself and saw the blue sea and the yachts, the awnings of the tavernas and the beach dotted with coloured umbrellas, that he gave up waiting.

'Ah, Mr Carmichael, in your country you have your system – Winston Churchill, Buckingham Palace, Rule Britannia – but here we do it differently, eh? Bam-bam! Everybody change! Bam-bam! Everybody change again! Ha! Why so solemn, Mr Carmichael, why so quiet? You are ill? You have a pain somewhere? Why not enjoy yourself? No one is stopping you from enjoying yourself. Why look over the hill when the view this way is so beautiful? *Kalí oreximas*, Mr Carmichael, *kalí thiaskedasímas*! The sensible man enjoys himself. What is the desire of every man? What is the duty of every man? To enjoy himself!'

HARRY

——

Dear Sophie. Someone has to be a witness, someone has to see. And tell? And tell? Tell me, Sophie, can it be a kindness not to tell what you see? And a blessing to be blind? And the best aid to human happiness that has ever been invented is a blanket made of soft, white lies?

I never knew that Dad knew about Anna. But that night – the men on the moon and Anna up on Olympus – our minds must have crossed paths. I said, 'There's something I want to know.' And after a long pause he said, 'Anna?' And I knew that he knew.

We had turned down the sound on the TV. The moon-men bobbed in silence over the Sea of Tranquillity.

He said, 'Yes, I knew about Anna.'

'But you didn't tell me.'

'I didn't know if you knew.'

'You were never going to tell me?'

(Sixteen years!)

'Would you have wanted me to? If you hadn't known?'

'The truth.'

'The truth!' He snorted, made a wry face and raised his whisky glass to his lips. Outside, it was getting light.

He said, 'You never told Sophie?'

'No.'

'And how did you know?'

'Because she told me. She – confessed. You know when she got the news about Uncle Spiro. The state she was in. It wasn't just – Before she left she said, "I've got something to tell you." She was crying. She said, "I'm pregnant."'

But I knew before that. I knew that summer, in Cornwall. Do you remember that day – the day you almost drowned? I already knew then.

I was sitting on the rug with Stella, half-way up the beach. She was getting out the things for our picnic and I was watching her emptying the bag, shooing away a fly. I never had any special feelings for Stella Irving. Just the usual jokey flirtation (jokey! Jesus!) that goes on when two couples are together. But that morning I could have reached across that rug and hugged her like my sister, because she looked so innocent, getting out those sandwiches and chicken legs, and I could see so clearly she didn't have an inkling.

You'd gone down to the water with Anna, and Frank had gone for some beers. It was hot. Blue sky, waves coming in lazily. Anna used to say that when the weather was like that it reminded her of Greece. She was holding your hands and making you float up in the water and kick your legs and you were both laughing.

Stella had a wide straw sun-hat. In a year's time she would be a mother too: her own daughter. As she bent over the picnic things, the brim of the hat hid her face and I looked at her breasts in her wet swim-suit. But I thought, even if she were stark naked beside me and we were the only ones on this beach, I wouldn't feel a scrap of lust for her. Just this need to hold her tight and say – God knows why – 'Sorry.'

She turned towards me and I looked away, and she said,

164

'You're quiet today, Harry.' But just as she said it, I wasn't quiet any more. I yelled, 'Jesus Christ!', or something like that, and jumped to my feet. Because I'd looked towards the water and I couldn't see you any more. I couldn't see you. I saw Anna, ten, fifteen yards out, with her head tilted back as if she were relishing the sensation of floating freely by herself. And then I saw the splash and thrash of your arms, some way to Anna's left, maybe five yards out. I didn't wait. I ran down the beach, plunged in and grabbed you.

Maybe I'd got it wrong. Maybe, as Anna said, my eyes had tricked me. (My eyes!) She said you'd learnt to do it – to float by yourself and splash your arms – and in any case you could still touch bottom there with your feet. We stood round the picnic rug, and I just kept repeating, 'She might have drowned! She might have drowned!' I was holding you and you were crying. Frank came down the beach with a string bag full of bottles of beer and lemonade, and I saw the way he checked, recognizing a crisis: 'What's happened?' Stella said, 'Sophie got into trouble in the water. Harry's just got her out.' His look changed, almost relaxed. 'Poor little Sophie,' he said, putting down the bottles. 'Poor little Sophie.' Anna said, 'She wasn't drowning, everyone. She was trying to swim.' Her face had this calm, sensible expression. Could she tell? Then she said to me, 'She's crying because you're holding her so tight. If you've just saved her from drowning, there's no need to suffocate her now.' She said this lightly, laughingly, without anger. I thought: She doesn't suspect. She picked up the beach towel and held it between her opened arms. 'Come here, Sophie. *Ela sti Mammásou.* Daddy just thought –' I thought: I could just hold on to you. Let her stand there like that with the towel and her arms emptily open. Then she'd know.

Her hair was wet and streaming and she was making a kissing shape with her lips. It was a decision, you see. For her sake. You were still crying and I really didn't want to let you go. But

165

I handed you over. And as soon as I did, you stopped crying. Then I knew I'd have to pretend. Silly Daddy. Made a silly mistake. Frightened little Sophie. Thought she was drowning.

But I really did think you were drowning. That's what I saw: my daughter drowning.

And it wasn't a mistake, either – I really saw what I saw, though I tried hard enough to make it something I hadn't seen, a trick of the eyes – when I went back to the hotel that previous afternoon.

She had already gone back, to lie down. A headache. The day had turned cloudy and sullen. Then Frank said, looking restless, that if nobody minded, he'd go and chase a ball around the course for a bit. He said, 'Be good, you two,' and winked. And Stella said, 'We've got our chaperone.' Pointing at you. Then, just a few moments after Frank had gone, she said, 'Damn! I left my book in the room.' And I said, 'That's okay. I'll get it. I'll see how Anna is, anyway.' I got up, brushing away the sand. I walked off, then stopped.

'Key?'

'Oh, they'll let you take it from the desk, won't they? Or you might still catch Frank.'

I suppose I did catch Frank.

Do you remember the zig-zagging path up the cliff? The wooden steps covered with sand? Slow going, with you. You'd want to be carried. Frank and I would toss a coin. The last bit through a tunnel of wind-curved trees. Then the hotel appearing, the flagpole on the lawn, and the view round the headland along the coast.

Frank's car was still in the car park. The big Rover. Our A40. We were like the poor relations in those days. Frank, the rising star of the Company. Me, the boss's renegade son. Though on that holiday, I think, everyone wondered. Frank wondered. Anna wondered. Did I wonder?

The key to Frank and Stella's room wasn't on its hook behind

166

the desk. Nor was their door locked. Not even properly shut. I still think about that casual omission. Then, of all times, not only to have not locked the door, but to have left it crassly resting on its latch. Did it mean that there had been no prior arrangements – she really did have a headache, he really had come to fetch his golf clubs – and that, as they might have said in some absurd scene of contrition, they had 'just got carried away'? Did that make it better, or worse? And supposing the door had been shut, and I had innocently knocked?

I stood outside and raised my knuckle. It was only that soft moan from inside that made me realize the door was not tightly closed. A moan so familiar and private, yet coming from another room. Perhaps I should have turned then on my heel, trod softly, numbly, automatically, back along that passageway, like a discreet hotel servant. But I did that later.

You have to see. I pushed the door an inch open with one finger. The head of the bed was hidden by the corner of a wardrobe. Was that luck of a kind? I didn't want to see her face. You have to see, but some things you can't look at. Her legs were round him. The curtains were drawn. Frank's arse, absurdly white where his swimming trunks went, was bucking up and down.

How long – a second? two seconds? – before I pulled the door softly to again? Should I have burst in? Action. Drama. Pieces flying everywhere. I thought: This is happening, before your eyes. Afterwards, you won't believe it. Take the picture.

Then I turned. Then I crept down the passage. Past other doors. Past our room. *Our* room? Number seven. Then I walked, like a sleep-walker, down the creaking staircase, holding the banister very tightly. Along the downstairs passage, past the lounge where they were serving cream teas, out on to the terrace where the sun was starting to break through again and the breeze was rattling the rope on the flagpole. And I was thinking all the time: This wasn't me. I'd left me behind. I had left my heart in a hotel in Cornwall. In an English seaside hotel with chintz armchairs and cream teas and dinner gongs. Locked it up and walked away. In a room in a holiday hotel where the sea air blew in and you could hear the waves at night and in the morning you could see fishing boats chugging out after lobsters, and Anna had said with a laugh, the first time we came, it was like a hotel in Agatha Christie, and our daughter slept in a little adjoining room with a party-door, so love-making had to be well timed and circumspect.

Past the flagpole. Down the zig-zagging steps. How long ago? How far away was this beach? There you were, kneeling by the rug, looking up. Stella being Mummy. I hadn't thought what to say. How my face might look. But Stella had this repentant expression, as if she understood something.

'Oh, I'm so sorry, Harry. It was here all the time. Right at the bottom of my bag.' And she held up a book. A well-thumbed paperback. On its cover, a couple in torn safari jackets, locked in torrid embrace.

'Did you see Frank?'

'No.'

'And how's Anna?'

He said, 'I never knew she was pregnant.'

'Only six weeks. She was going – she told me this – to get rid of it. Then she got that telegram from Greece. There wasn't any time. She hadn't seen her uncle for seven years.'

'And that was the first you knew about it?'

'Yes. How did *you* know? She told you?'

He eyed his glass.

'No. Let's just say I knew. Saw what I saw.' We looked at each other. 'You were away so much, don't forget. Taking pictures.'

I thought: You old bastard.

168

'Yes, I was away. Which is how I knew it couldn't have been me who made her pregnant.'

'And as I recall, you were even more eager, that winter, to get as far away as possible. The further, the better. The more dangerous, the better. You never thought of telling me?'

'That's immaterial now. Why didn't *you* tell *me*?'

He lowered his eyes. Raised them again.

He said, 'All the same, why did you never tell me?'

'She was dead, wasn't she?'

He held his gaze on me. I didn't say anything. Maybe he saw my thought – or, rather, that I didn't have the thought he was looking for. Maybe he was looking for more than one thought.

'Frank?' he said.

'I could put that same point to you too, couldn't I? I never did a thing. What do you think he thinks – that nobody ever found out?' I laughed. 'Oh, I wanted to kill him. That's all. I mean, spectacularly kill him. I still have this fantasy. Like to hear it? I'm in this plane. Just me, the plane, and one bomb for Frank. One bomb. I'm coming in low over Surrey. I'm homing in on Frank's house. It's a Sunday morning and he's at home. He runs out on to his lawn, and first he thinks it's a joke, then he throws up his hands in horror. I fire my guns, just to let him know it's business. Then I swoop down and let the bomb go smack into him.'

He wasn't shocked by this. Nor did he smile. He said, with a poker face, 'You know, I have to consider the security of my senior executives.'

'Especially in your business.'

'Especially in my business.'

'Don't worry. The revenge is already taken care of. He's where I never wanted to be, isn't he?'

He said, 'I know.'

169

Then he said, 'But there's no logic in that, you know. He's in his element. He knows a damn sight more about the Company now than I do. He's a good MD. He'll be a good chairman.'

'But you'd rather have had me?'

'No. I don't feel that now. Not now.'

He looked at the silent pictures on the TV.

He said, 'You know, if someone had said to me when I was ten years old that in my lifetime men would land on the moon – not only that, but I'd watch them do it – I'd have said they were mad.'

I said, 'How do we know they're really there? It could all be happening in some studio mock-up. It could all be a trick to con the Russians. To know, you'd have to go yourself.'

'I mean it, Harry. He knows more about it than I do. It's not simple stuff any more.'

'You mean, not nice, clean, simple ways of killing people?'

He said nothing. As if he hadn't heard. Perhaps he thought: This is an old routine. We've been through this routine before.

He said, 'Let's get some air.'

We opened the French windows. The garden was still. A slight rustling in the trees. The moon had disappeared and the sun was just catching the tops of the cedars. A scent of honeysuckle. I thought: Four weeks ago I was with the Marines in the A Shau, in the wake of the Hamburger Hill carnage. Fucked-up and far from home. Or, as one hollow-faced Marine lieutenant, who was at the frivolous stage, put it: Dug-in, doped-up, demoralized or dead. They were still there now, like the men on the moon who we couldn't see, though we could stare at the sky. And I was in a Surrey garden.

We strolled to the end of the terrace. As we turned, I wanted to do that simple but rare thing and take his arm. He had been on my right, so now was on my left. But just for a moment I forgot and my hand felt the hard metal beneath his sleeve. I suppose he felt nothing. But perhaps in that ever-replaced

170

arm, over the years, he had developed some obscure sense of touch.

He said, 'I've never told you, have I?'

ANNA

Dear Harry. Dear husband Harry . . .

I was born in Drama. But I was brought up in Paradise.
Though they say that it's all spoilt now. Even Thassos. The
tourists have come and invaded, each one of them wanting
their piece of paradise, and you wouldn't recognize now, as you
wouldn't recognize a thousand places in Greece, the little bay
and the hollow in the hillside amongst the pines where, when
my uncle first saw it there was only a solitary summer-house
with its weathered stucco and balcony, its terraced garden, its
well under a canopy of vines, and the name above the lintel,
chosen back in Turkish times by my Aunt Panayiota's first
husband, who must have been a happy, uninventive man: 'The
Villa Paradise'.

But paradise is never where you think. It's always somewhere
you once were and never knew at the time, or somewhere you
never guessed you might find it. And Uncle Spiro never
thought that his villa was paradise, even before the war. He
thought paradise was England.

Paradise was once a shabby apartment off a street called
Küfergasse in the middle of a ruined city. And yet you never
knew how often, in that room where we found so much joy, I

had wept. Not for the fate of mankind. Though I suppose people must have wept for that, in Nuremberg. But for the fate of Anna Vouatsis, orphan and virgin of one-and-twenty, who had made her way all alone – clutching the credentials of an official translator to the International Military Tribunal, afraid of bandits, afraid of her own conscience – from the country of her birth, where (but this was her secret) she never intended to return.

Happiness is like a fall of snow, it smooths and blanks out all there was before it. And, yes, everything is relative, and my complaints were nothing to what you could find in those Nuremberg depositions. But you never quite understood – with all your keen-sightedness, with all your professional interest in the world's troubles – how your Anna, your very own Anna, was one of the world's walking wounded.

Not that I blame you. How can I do that? I am the one to blame. I am the one to blame. But I won't ever forget that happiness. Don't mistake that. That snowfall of happiness. Switzerland, the white mountains, and those first four years. With Frank it wasn't happiness. It was a tactical affair. A tactical desertion.

Such a tough little bitch was sitting somewhere inside me, while the rest of me was ready to melt. In Nuremberg, adding my own little contribution to the paperwork of grief, I understood what the war had done to me. It had made me a thick-skinned, old-young thing, with a limited capacity for outrage and for assimilating the ills of the universe. When you told me about Robert, when you said he made bombs, I let the words wash right over me. I said to myself: That has nothing to do with anything. When we drove that first time through those gates at Hyfield and up that gravel drive, I didn't see any bombs. I saw the fairy-tales my Uncle Spiro had told me coming true. When you said – oh, with such wary pride – 'Dad, this is Anna,' I didn't see a monster. I saw a perfect English gentleman.

And in any case, I think, someone has to make them. Maybe we just need them, for our safety and protection and to guard the things we love. People hurt easily, they need armour. And if they hadn't dropped bombs on Nuremberg, we might never have all been there, to mete out justice and put the world to rights. And you and I, Harry, might never have met.

At first I thought that I would change your mind – that I *had* changed your mind. Then that Sophie would change your mind. Then –

And what I never told you is that *he* knew. I mean Robert. Even wanted it to happen. Oh, only so far. Just so you would feel a touch of persuasive jealousy. He never stopped wanting you back. 'Into the fold', as he put it. Never promised Frank anything. And he must have known he had an ally in me that very first time we met. He smiled so welcomingly. He took my coat so graciously and chivalrously. It was like some scene in one of those films that Uncle Spiro used to take me to see before the war, in Salonika. It surprised me that he used both arms. Then he led us in (a log fire! Oak panels!), and it was as though he were ushering me into some home that, he knew, had been waiting for me all my life.

He knew. But you never guessed. With your eyes always straying, like some person guilty of your own happiness, to the window that looked out on the world. Couldn't see what was under your nose.

It's funny how what I always remember are the winters, though people – English people – used to say, It must be wonderful – coming from somewhere so sunny! When you live on an island in wartime, it's like being wrapped in a shroud – is it better or worse to be cut off from the mainland of events? And when the rain and mist moved in from Thrace it was as though the world was obliterated: now anything could happen here, and no one would know.

Once, as if a veil had been lifted, we saw two, three warships,

175

solidifying out of the gloom, beating westwards through the drizzle. They came close enough so you could see the water pluming off their bows and the outlines of their guns. They looked so beautiful. So heroic! Uncle Spiro said they must be Italian ships. Or Italian ships commandeered by the Germans. Because by now the British would surely have trounced the Italians. They were too fast, too modern-looking to be Bulgarian. They couldn't be Turkish. We were down on the beach gathering driftwood, and we forgot the cold and our hunger. We argued, long after they'd disappeared, knowing nothing about ships, over whether they were destroyers or frigates or corvettes or minelayers. It was strange, that rapt animation, as if to hide our disappointment.

Because the main thing was, they weren't British ships. If they'd been British, we would have known about it beforehand. And they would have steamed right into the bay to rescue us.

Uncle Spiro used to say: 'Greece was once the cradle of civilization, but what is Greece now?' He would pick up a handful of stones or dust. 'Greece is this' – he would empty his hand. 'And Greece is this' – he would rub his thumb, in the gesture of crude greed, against his fingertips. And we were not even Greeks! We were Macedonians. Miserable Macedonia! Quarrelled over by Turks and Bulgars and Serbs, and chopped about by the Big Powers. 'You know what the French mean, little Anna, when they say "Macedonia"? They mean "fruit salad"!' My grandfathers and great-grandfathers had fought in those bitter little wars that the Great War had swallowed up. No wonder the latest generation, who could officially call themselves Greek, had the minds of brigands. Feuding with each other over piles of tobacco, waiting for the brown leaves to turn into banknotes.

He had told them as much, recklessly, as a young man with scholarly ambitions. And they had said, 'Very well, if you must, go and become an educated man, but don't come knocking on the door when you are starving.' But he'd surprised them all. Found his way to far-away London, even seen the tranquil lawns of Oxford and Cambridge. Then returned to marry a rich widow – Aunt Panayiota, whom I can't recall – who in turn had left him a rich widower, strolling the *paralía* in Salonika, in finely cut English suits. It was *they* who had had to humble themselves before him, even permitting their little jewel, their late, unexpected blessing, Anna, to spend summers with him at his villa on Thassos. Until that warehouse fire which had left Anna parentless, after which Uncle Spiro became her permanent guardian.

That fire, he told me, after a year or two had passed and he knew that my feelings for my dead parents were of a kind with his for my dead aunt, was arson, no mistaking. Though it had never been proved. An act of mercantile vandalism that had gone further than was intended. Ha! The nemesis of the Vouatsis! Burnt by their own tobacco! Greed and brigandry! But he spoke more softly and more carefully when my older brothers, Sotiri and Manoli, were killed within six months of each other, one in Albania and one on the Aliakmon.

What did I do in the war? I lived in Paradise. And never knew it. I spent the war in a summer villa. Though during the hot, blue, harsh days of summer I dreamed of cool, green England. Of fleecy English skies and English meadows and English willows draped over the cool Thames. And during the winters I dreamed of English tea-times on winter evenings, beside roaring fires and brass fenders in solid brick houses (you recognize what were once my dreams?), with toast and tea-cakes and scones and muffins (I learnt all the words) and anything else Uncle Spiro's memory could muster or his own dreams invent, while the wind howled round the Villa Paradise and our stomachs gnawed on hunger and dread.

What did I do in the war? I learnt English. A dangerous thing to have done, given the circumstances. Whole evenings, whole days sometimes, when we would speak to each other only in English. With Uncle Spiro I read Shakespeare and Wordsworth and Doctor Johnson. And at first I really thought that this devotedness would make it all be over sooner. It was like a prayer. It would make the British hurry so much more to save us.

He said they would come. It wouldn't be long. He said this in '41. But they hadn't come. They'd got out of Greece altogether. But only, so he said, so they could return in proper strength. Before the last war, when he was a boy, British policemen had come to Drama to show the Turks how things were done. And in 1916, the British had cleared the Bulgars out of Macedonia in two weeks – and they'd never have been there in the first place if it hadn't been for that fool King Constantine.

They'd come in submarines. Or they'd come dropping out of the sky on thousands of parachutes. They had the finest navy and army in the world and would make short work of it. The British were a peace-loving people who cherished fairness and freedom, but, like the ancient Athenians, they understood the value of military strength to preserve those very things. The British were the most civilized nation on earth. That was why they had ruled half of it. They were so civilized that they studied and revered our ancient past, while we let our temples crumble and destroyed ourselves with our eternal bickering and ignorance.

What did I do in the war? I was lucky, amazingly lucky. I held on to my luck. First there was a German garrison, then the Bulgars. If there had been a choice, we would have chosen the Germans. Some things I never told you, Harry, you learn to wipe them out. I stayed a virgin. At an age when I knew I was becoming beautiful, I learnt to make myself look ugly. At an age when I knew I was growing up, I learnt to turn myself into a perpetual, stunted child – Uncle's little niece whom no one dare touch. I wasn't raped or sent to the brothels in Kavalla.

We weren't made homeless. Uncle Spiro wasn't mutilated or shipped off to a labour camp.

But I knew that if they searched the villa and found even that small handful of English books that he brought with him from Salonika, they could decide to shoot us. Shoot us, like they shot the three men who hung one evening, heads down, from the plane tree in the village square. They had been shot many times. You could see that. And three the next evening, and three the evening after that.

I used to think if I took the books and burnt them or bundled them up and threw them in the sea, then perhaps I would be saving our lives. But then if I threw them away I would be throwing away the one thing that made those months after months on that island endurable, which gave them some thin, vicarious purpose. And, again, if I threw them away, perhaps we would only deserve it if the British never came.

But they did come. In the autumn of '44. The Germans and the Bulgars departed. So then it was all right for the Greeks to fight each other . . .

I said I didn't want to leave him. I would soon be back. Before the winter. But I think I knew, as we stood on that railway platform, that I wouldn't return. One English watchword he could never convert into reality was 'stiff upper lip'. He was a Greek. His face contorted. His eyes streamed with farewell emotion. And I saw how when I was gone he would start to think, achingly, of how glad and proud he'd been looking after me, my gallant guardian, in what, now it was over, now new troubles were coming, might start to seem again like Paradise.

Yet it was I who, just as much – more – had looked after him. And he saw that too. I was twenty-one. I didn't want to become a nurse.

He was just fifty-three then. Though he looked older. His career of scholarship had been brought to a halt in what should have been its prime years, and, now, there was little chance of his picking up again the pieces of his former life.

Pneumonia? Or a broken heart?

The station hall was full of slogans and posters. People clutching all they possessed.

Of course, he didn't know that my journey would take me, eventually, to England. So as compensation for having lost me he would have the knowledge that I had settled in the land of his dreams – as if all that training he had given me in the war had borne fruit. His niece – an Englishwoman! That I would write him letters like the fulfilment of wishes – he is even called Harry ('God for Harry! . . .'); there is this house in Surrey – yet which remained strangely vague about what my husband did (a 'journalist') or what my father-in-law did, and never mentioned, before the letters got less frequent and finally stopped altogether, what must have been obvious to both of us, especially given what was happening in Greece – that he might have come to England too. Perhaps he would not dare suggest it, till I did. Perhaps he had become disaffected with the British now they were, in reality, the arbitrators of Greece. Or perhaps he had come to feel, as prematurely old men may feel, that this was his country, he was born in it, and he would die in it, even though it was a mess.

They were still fighting when Sophie was born. I used to skip the reports in the English papers. And to think you very nearly went out there – to take photographs!

But I think he knew. I think he saw it all, unblurred by those farewell tears. More than one kind of desertion.

More than one kind of desertion. Dear Harry. If it hadn't been for that sudden telegram, you might never have known at all – my confession spilling out with my own farewell (farewell!) tears. Because we'd made up our minds. I would get rid of it. Go to someone. While you were away. Then we'd stop. And say nothing. Before two homes got broken.

In the plane to Athens I thought, I want this journey never to stop. I want to stay up here for ever. I have nowhere to go. No home. No one to forgive me. When we landed, there wasn't even any of that famous Greek sunshine. It was raining. The custodial faces of King Paul and Marshal Papagos looked down at me in the arrival hall. I was suddenly shocked to be where I was. To be speaking my own language to my own people. Shocked by the beggars and touts, the jumble and disrepair of the streets and all the signs of a country crawling out from a decade of misery. In England it was Coronation year, and Frank had said the best was yet to come. Shocked to be in the capital city of the land of my birth, where I had never been before and where I felt a total stranger. Shocked by the sudden sight of the Parthenon, bony white against the grey sky, as if I had never expected it would be there. I booked into a hotel for the night and thought of that girl arriving in Nuremberg. It was all like a reproof. I thought: I should get rid of it here, somehow, here in this country. I phoned the hospital in Salonika and they said there was little time. It was still raining the next morning when I took the plane north. The sky was dark with clouds and I thought: Even the gods are angry.

SOPHIE

———

Brooklyn. 'Broken Land'. Somebody told me, Doctor K. that's just what it means.

Every so often I still go up to the Heights, above the Expressway, just to look at that mirage of Manhattan across the water. The views in this place still knock me out, even though I'm no longer a goggle-eyed Limey. They still give me a kick. And do you know what's so great about them? It's that they're absolutely man-made, they're as man-made as you're ever going to get. All steel and concrete and lights and lines and glass and electricity. But they aren't human. That's the big kick, that's the come-on. It's pure man-made, but it ain't human. Oh sure, the humans are *there*, never so many of them, never so packed together, milling around under the towers like ants under lifted stones. But you have to get up real close before you see them, you have to get through all the glass and concrete superstructure before you feel their hot, below-decks breath. Or else it's the other way round: you're down there at people-level, amongst the voices and faces and the fogged-up windows and the smell of coffee and pizza, then you step out and say to yourself, Wow, I'd almost forgotten: there's this *edifice*.

How many lives can you see at a glance in New York, without

183

seeing a single life? Supposing every window were a life – a little bright box of life.

A man is six feet tall (okay, *you're* not – but you can handle that) and the Citicorp building is nine hundred feet. There's got to be something wrong there. Or else something splendid, something sublime.

Just stand back and take in the view. You think this is one brute of a city, but it's also magic, it's amazement to the eye. Distance lends enchantment. Is that the name of the game? The trick of it? To rise above it all. To get a little vantage, a little perspective, a little elevation. To perch at some perfect window (say, the twenty-second floor, somewhere around 59th and Park) with your perfectly chilled Martini, and reduce it all to a vision.

Am I a hypocrite? I think little boys shouldn't play with toy guns, but I think Leonidas, holding the pass with his Spartans, was a fine, brave thing. And once I read Homer because I was told Homer was the greatest. But what else was Homer singing about so deathlessly than these guys with spears sending other guys down to Hades?

Distance lends enchantment. And time heals. That's the other big sop, the other big lie. Let some years go by. Oh, five, ten years. Then rub your finger over the place where the old wound was. See? Hardly feel a thing.

You know, the boys came in from school the other day and Paul says, 'Mom, can you tell me something? Is the world getting bigger or smaller?' Just like that. I didn't know if it was some joke with a trick answer, or something their teacher had thrown out at them, or something going round the schoolyard, or else some serious, anxious inquiry. I said, 'I don't think I know that. But I guess *you* must be getting bigger, though!' And I put my arms round him, and I felt him wriggle like mad, the way they both do these days, to get free.

So tell me, Doctor K. What do I do? Do I answer his letter? Do I go to see him? Or do I stay here with you?

HARRY

——

Last night Jenny and I watched on the news the Task Force steaming its way towards the South Atlantic. Those by now familiar shots of troops jogging round the decks of a requisitioned liner and helicopters waltzing over the waves have lost their vague air of comedy. As if, though it could all still be called off at any moment (what do they say in the States, Sophie – it will happen? It won't?), the imperceptible point has already been passed when the pressure of feeling that has all along been, secretly, wanting it to happen, willing it to happen, has outweighed the pressure of feeling that says: But this is preposterous.

A show-case war. An exhibition war. A last little war for old time's sake. Sending the ships and the men to some far-off corner of the globe, while the nation waits and guesses. Save that this time, along with the ships and the men, goes a small battalion of camera crews and newsmen, and, despite what they say about the difficulties, at that range, of satellite transmission, it is going to be the TV event of the year.

And it's strange to think that I could be there. True, I'm sixty-four, but I'm a fit man, my eye's still good. (And I feel young, absurdly young.) They would give me a flak-jacket and a helmet. They would pay me the slightly begrudging respect due to some worthy veteran. But (thank God!) no editor or one-time crony has phoned me up actually to suggest it. How about it, Harry? And what have you been doing for these last ten years anyway? What do you say? For old time's sake?

For old time's sake! Those scenes at Portsmouth! That pantomime! That performance! How everyone played their parts. The troops lining the rails. The bands, the cheers, the ships' hooters, the women waving and weeping. It wasn't even a re-run, with twentieth-century props, of grand Victorian send-offs for illustrious imperial expeditions. It was the Trojan War all over again. Someone had raped our precious Falkland Isles, so the ships must sail. And somewhere, in a sacred grove, behind the harbour, before the bands could strike up and the ships slip their cables, someone had discreetly cut the throat of a modern-day Iphigeneia.

Iphigeneia! Iphigeneia! Of all those old Greek myths that my Uncle Edward once made his special province, it is that one that sticks with me. The blue bay at Aulis, flecked with white-caps. The ships beached, pinned down by the wind, the troops grumbling and mutinous. And Iphigeneia on the altar.

It's so easy to imagine how it might have happened otherwise. How Agamemnon might have said, No thanks – nothing is worth *that*. How he might have embraced his daughter and said to his men, Okay, enough, let's go home. The wind would have held. The Trojan War would have been cancelled. Instead of sailing to a ten-year blood-bath, the men might have enjoyed a heaven-sent interlude. A seaside break. Beach games, cooled by that onshore breeze. Like those paratroopers parading on the sun-decks of the *Canberra*: a holiday cruise after all.

She wants me to take real photos again. But she wants me to take only beautiful pictures. The sun burnishing the wind-bent grass on a Wiltshire hillside. Her own face. On those nights when we first went to bed together it was as though there were certain things which, in spite of herself, she had to broach. As if there were ghosts she thought she would quickly exorcize, but she found them more stubborn than she supposed. When you are sixty-four you cannot pretend that you have no past. She would kiss the scar on my cheek, cautiously at first and then lingeringly, running her lip, the tip of her tongue along it, as if she had found some new, unexpected erogenous zone. She would say: 'Tell me about . . .' and 'What was it like . . .' And even: 'Did you ever – just a little bit – enjoy it?' Then she asked (ten years ago she was only *thirteen*): 'And why did you stop?'

No Trojan War. No Homer. No ten-year siege. No wooden horse. No Hector, Achilles, Andromache, Hecuba. No story. No action. No news. (On news-stands throughout Hellas, words to make an old hack weep: 'Trojan Task Force Recalled'.)

I used to believe once that ours was the age in which we would say farewell to myths and legends, when they would fall off us like useless plumage and we would see ourselves clearly only as what we are. I thought the camera was the key to this process. But I think the world cannot bear to be only what it is. The world always wants another world, a shadow, an echo, a model of itself. I think of Uncle Edward, the bright hope of New College, who marched off to war in 1915, his head full of the words and deeds of the Greeks and Romans and the myths with which they had filled their own heads. Who knows if that other world in his head made it harder or easier for him to bear (for just that short, long while) what he found?

When I was a boy I was taught by the same ageing classics master who had taught my uncle. Mr Vere. 'Percy' Vere. The schoolboy game was to count the number of times (surprisingly many) he had scrupulously to avoid saying 'persevere'. We were urged to 'persist', to 'soldier on'. I think I was aware that he saw in me some potential reincarnation of his former glorious protégé. If I 'stuck to it', he would say, as we struggled with Aeschylus, I would 'enter another world'. '*Agamemnon*, the opening chorus: the old men of Argos describe the scene at Aulis. Beech, would you start us off?' But I disappointed him. And my uncle's memory. And as for entering another world, I found I could do that more easily by stepping into the Rex, the Empire or the Rialto cinemas. Where, though it's conceivable I may have taken a more than average interest in the camera-work, I used also to imagine, like any adolescent schoolboy in similar circumstances, that Harlow or Lombard might step down from the screen to place themselves in positions of intimate proximity to me, or alternatively that I might be wafted up to take over the invincible roles of Gary Cooper or Douglas Fairbanks Junior.

I think the cinema replaced the vision of Greece and Rome. The era of classical education did not die, quite, with my uncle at the Battle of Loos, but it perished during the rise of the talking picture. Once, privileged generations were brought up to emulate a world no one could see. Now everyone had a world to emulate, floating before them.

You emerge from the cinema (it is called, perhaps, the Odeon or the Doric and is done up with fake Greek columns). Just for a while you possess an aura, a power, a stature. Your feet lift a little from the ground. It is a place for erotic training: the darkness, the clinches on the screen – what more instruction do you need? And how did you learn to walk, to stare, to stroke your jaw, to light your cigarette or toss it aside, in just that way? You learnt it from the movies.

In those days a newsreel was always a standard feature of the programme. Dressed up with inane music and plum-voiced commentaries, it was nonetheless a reminder that there was a real world as well as the faked one in which people moved with Hollywood stylization. Now, they no longer show news-reels in cinemas, but the movies you see aspire to the 'actuality' of the newsreel, while TV can never have enough 'real life' footage. So that it's no longer easy to distinguish the real from the fake, or the world on the screen from the world off it.

In Vietnam it was common: 'I don't like this movie. Get me out of this movie. Someone, for Chrissakes, cut this SCENE!'

And it goes without saying that a task force of cameras should accompany the Task Force to the Falklands. As if without them it could not take place.

When did it happen? That imperceptible inversion. As if the camera no longer recorded but conferred reality. As if the world were the lost property of the camera. As if the world wanted to be claimed and possessed by the camera. To translate itself, as if afraid it might otherwise vanish, into the new myth of its own authentic-synthetic photographic memory.

As if it were a kind of comfort that every random, crazy thing that gets done should be monitored by some all-seeing, unfeeling, inhuman eye.

Not to be watched. Isn't that a greater fear than the fear of being watched?

In the earliest portrait photographs everyone is *posing*. Un-selfconsciously striking Sunday-best, rhetorical attitudes, as if they do not yet know what a camera is – they think of it as some swayable human audience and they have a sense of themselves as belonging to some proud theatre. Then at some forlorn time posing got discredited. It started to seem embarrassing, artificial. And the cry of the photographer became that insistent, exasperated and paradoxical demand: 'Act naturally please.'

How did this happen? And when? In 1918? In 1945? And what does that mean: to *act* naturally?

He nods his helmeted head. Agamemnon, leader of men. Does (naturally) what a man has to do. Says yes to war, myth, action, news, classical literature, the death of his daughter. Acts unnaturally.

I know it's absurd, I know it's unreal. Up here, in the Cessna, while she sits below the control tower, listening to Derek's yarns, it's as if there's some invisible cord between us, like those model aeroplanes and their remote-control operators up on Epsom Downs. I know it's a dream, it's impossible, and one part of me was always ready for it suddenly to finish. Except now there's something which can't be undone. That first time in the plane, it wasn't air-sickness. She told me that same day. She must have struggled to sound neutral, and my silence must have been blatant and cruel as murder. The mother not the child. (Prepare the words: 'I think it would be better if –') Then I saw that her face was awash with tears. 'I want you to *marry* me,' she said. That's when it got deeper than deep, and beyond a dream.

I know it's absurd. If I didn't know her better, I might say she was too young to know better, and if I knew myself better, I might say I was too old not to know better.

But I don't want to lose her. I don't want to lose her.

SOPHIE

So, my darlings, we will go to England. We will get the plane, just you and me, to England. To see your grandfather.

What is it like? It's where you come from in a way, it's where you *were*, but of course you won't remember it. And maybe it's no longer the way I remember it. Or rather, the way I remember it is like it never was.

England is green and cool and damp and old and crooked. Look at the map. England is like a little hunched-up old lady at the seaside, her back turned towards the rest of Europe, dipping her toe into the Atlantic Ocean and pulling up her skirts round her shrivelled body. She is sitting down because she is no longer steady on her legs. Someone has thrown in her direction a two-tone beach-ball called Ireland and she is screwing up her face in displeasure.

You wouldn't believe that she was once a big, plump, bossy Empress. And you wouldn't believe that even now, in 1982, there is a fleet of ships sailing off to fight, on behalf of this little old lady, for some even tinier islands on the other side of the world.

England is small. When we get there everything will seem as if it was built on a different scale, the house, the streets, the

191

cars. And you'll see all those things you've only seen so far in pictures – castles, Beefeaters, funny red buses. So it will seem that England is really only a toy country. But you mustn't believe that. That things are just toys.

We'll get the plane, my angels. You'll have to look after your mother, like two grown-up young men. It's a big journey for me, you see – perhaps even bigger for me than for you. Going back can be the hardest journey. And perhaps, if I haven't done so before then, that's when I'll tell you, up in the plane, high over the ocean. I'll say: Once, in England . . .

He said, yes of course I should go. Take the boys too. Yes, it was the right, the proper, the best thing to do. He was smiling, as if he were truly happy for me. I showed him the letter. And I said, I want to go. He said, No, he wouldn't come himself. It would be right at his busy time of the year, and he got enough trips to England, on business, didn't he? And, in any case, it was right that just – He kept smiling. He always knew how to smile. He said he'd fix up our flights. Half price. And then I asked him, but what did he think, actually think – about Harry getting married again. And he said he thought it was crazy. Just plain crazy.

And then he said: 'You mean the world to me.'

HARRY

———

Peter says there is always a mark. Though it may not be easy to detect. No matter how much time elapses. Once the soil has been moved. Once men have interfered with the earth: it never reverts, there is always a mark.

An out-of-work actor, in jeans and old sweater. A hopeful Aladdin, putting his trust in the magic lamp of the camera. He is infatuated with the life and death of people he will never know, buried for over three thousand years beneath the ground. He gives me elementary briefings in prehistory. Almost certainly, the Bronze Age Britons had trading links with Mycenaean Greece. If Homer's heroes ever really lived, they would have lived at the time the Bronze Age flourished in Britain.

But we are unlucky with 880390 to 960370. No spectral field systems loom into vision. He is undiscouraged. Another time. When the grass is higher, after a heavier rainfall, in a different light. It is a canny business, this hunting of the Bronze Age, like tracking some inordinately shy animal. He tells Michael to make one more circuit and tells me to keep snapping (because it can happen sometimes: the eye can't see ghosts but the camera can).

And yet there will be something to celebrate. When we're

193

back at the airfield. When we've landed and we're all together in Derek's den. Our little agreement. 'Listen everyone, Jenny and I have got something to tell you.'

We fly over the Wylye valley, across the southern fringe of the Plain to the Avon, then north towards Pewsey. Over our right shoulders, the spire of Salisbury Cathedral.

I know this landscape is a lie. Skin deep. Hedgerowed, church-towered, village-strewn England. Rub the map and civilization as we know it disappears. The Bronze Age emerges. And Peter would be the first to point out that these vistas which we like to think of as virgin, naked countryside, the bare bosoms of hills and little pubic clumps of woodland, are all – if it has taken millennia – man-made.

And rub the map again – ever so lightly this time – and a less benign illusion dissolves itself. Half of Wiltshire and Dorset, good lumps of Hampshire and Berkshire are military property. M.O.D. Keep Out. Not countryside any more – camouflage. When I first took up aerial photography I was amazed at the number of mysterious installations, hidden at ground level and unmarked on Ordnance Survey maps, which, quite apart from the more or less advertised air bases and training areas, could be seen from the air. As if, wheeling overhead in a Cessna with a camera, you ran the risk of being taken for a spy.

When I told Peter about these bird's-eye revelations, he nodded, unsurprised, as if his own experience of archaeological espionage had led to the same discovery. He said, 'But it's nothing new. Look at a map of Bronze Age Britain, and what would stand out most prominently? Camps, forts, defence works. What was the great invention of the Bronze Age? The technology of warfare. The sword. That went out only in the last century. Strictly speaking, we're still living in the Iron Age . . .'

We forgot the men on the moon. We came in from the terrace.

194

He poured more whisky and he said, 'And I was the *lucky* one. The lucky one! I never asked to be head of BMC. You know that, don't you? You've worked it all out, haven't you? You know that I wished I'd been killed instead of Richard and Edward, don't you?'

One morning in March, Sophie, which must have been a very noisy and confused morning, in 1918, my father was standing in a trench in northern Picardy, when a grenade landed just a few paces away from him. This was near the town of Albert, ten miles north of the Somme, but at that time it must have seemed like nowhere on earth. The grenade, which landed some five yards from my father, happened also to land less than a foot from his commanding officer, who was lying at the time, unconscious and immobilized from a previous explosion, on the floor of the trench. My father ran to the grenade, picked it up, turned to throw it clear, and, as he did so, it exploded and blew off his arm.

There might be several interpretations of this event. One might be, judging from the criterion of self-preservation, that it was an act of unqualified stupidity. Another, which was the verdict of the army, upheld by eye-witnesses and by the C.O., who, though technically no witness, had every reason to take a highly commendatory view, was that it was an act of unquestionable heroism, meriting nothing less than a Victoria Cross.

I can – just about – imagine a third version, in which my father is less the agent of his own volition than the puppet of conditioned reflexes and received ideas. Remember this is 1918 and the world is only just aware of how it has slid into the twentieth century. He sees the grenade fall and wishes it did not pose him its terrible moral choice. But given that it does, a whole set of notions that have been drummed into his twenty years counters the instinct in his stomach to bolt for cover – duty, training, his brothers' names on the Roll of Honour, the shame of appearing cowardly, even some half-remembered image, drawn in his case not from Hollywood but perhaps from some ink-blotched school-book (he sees himself as one of the three Horatii or as Ajax bestriding the body of Patroclus), and he finds himself running like an automaton towards the grenade.

But I did not believe this version. My father, who was by this time Captain Beech, had been too long at the front – a miraculously unscathed fifteen months – to be duped in this way. And, besides, since that night at Hyfield, I have known differently.

And I have never told anyone. Even when he died and the press were making hay – Death of a Hero, and variations on that theme – I never breathed a word.

Everyone has their picture of the Great War. Somewhere in the picture is a horrific collision of the antiquated and the modern. A cavalry charge into the teeth of machine-guns. It was not the first or last, if it was the biggest of such collisions, but only the terrible prototype, perhaps, of further collisions that would go on happening, in even more polarized and gro-tesque forms. As when the latest in military science flattens overnight the fabric of ancient cities or consumes in balls of sticky fire the thatch and daub of a South-east Asian village. Or when the modern photo-explorer sets out to 'capture on film' (before he disappears!) the remote tribesman who can still be found living in pre-Bronze Age conditions. (And the tribesman says, No thanks: the camera will steal his reality.)

One picture of the Great War is of two countries, England and France, separated, physically, by a distance so small that the sounds of warfare could carry from one to the other, yet separated, mentally, by a gulf as big as that from the earth to the moon. You think of a traffic, in one direction, of un-suspecting men, and a traffic, in the other, of cruel telegrams. But you forget that sometimes the traffic was reversed and that telegrams now and then brought to the men at the front the news of ordinary, domestic calamity.

196

He lost his arm on March 30th, 1918. I was born on the 27th. What I never knew was that he knew *before*. On a March afternoon, about to go up to the line, he hears that his wife has died, giving birth to a son. And the morning after he receives this news, a grenade falls into his path, which the highest principles of valour, at least, demand he pick up.

He said it was a common thing – it happened all the time. The grenades sometimes took ten seconds to explode and they were usually thrown too soon. He said he never deserved to get the V.C. and he would never have got it if he hadn't lost his arm.

No camera, of course, was present to record exactly what happened. To show, for example, how long he held on to the grenade after picking it up, how far he ran with it (but why should he have done that?) along the trench, or how soon after leaving his hand it exploded. But what no camera could show and what he himself could not tell was whether there had been some instant of teetering, agonized indecision – when the intention was defeated, when he stepped out of the picture and the picture changed, and with a bang, instead of being scattered into nothingness, the whole pattern of his future life clamped around him.

A change of roles. Richard, the eldest and heir-apparent to the family business. Edward, the budding scholar, the family indulgence. Robert, the – ?

He said he was that stock, stage figure – the nincompoop youngest son. Except that in those days they really used to exist. He said he never minded being a nincompoop youngest son, that was fine by him. Sandhurst was full of nincompoop youngest sons who had 'What-shall-we-do-with-him?' stamped all over them. Some of them got ambitious and became insufferable, and some of them never even knew they were nincompoops.

What she had liked about him was that he did know, and

didn't mind – he was a wise nincompoop. And he would never have guessed that a nincompoop could turn out to be so lucky – or become so serious.

Their short marriage began in April 1917. They honeymooned in Somerset, near Minehead – away from the English Channel. In a country cottage.

He said when he came home on leave he never knew what to tell her. He didn't know how to tell her. What he used to say was, It was worse for the horses.

He said there was no logic. Richard and Edward being volunteers and getting killed, Richard at Neuve Chapelle and Edward at Loos, while he was still a cadet. And him being a regular officer and surviving.

He came out of the Great War in 1918, minus a wife, minus two brothers and minus an arm. But he had acquired the rank of Major, a Victoria Cross, and a son whom, because of periods of hospitalization, he scarcely saw for the first year of that son's life, but whom, in any case, or so the son would later surmise, he had no special wish to see at all. He was in his early twenties but he was already a middle-aged man. He was also, since his two brothers were dead, the sole heir to the family business. And, given the nature of that business, and the business of the world in the previous few years, he was also about to be rich.

In 1923, one year after the death of his father, with the intention of adopting the obsolescent, crusty old style of a sort of squire without a manor, he bought Hyfield House, a Queen Anne building in Surrey, with its own driveway, gardens, orchard and paddock. No one saw through this pose to a former youthful nincompoop. Absence of a limb and the possession of a false one had conferred on him a mysterious solidity and integrity. He never remarried. He sent his son to boarding school. He engaged in public tasks. He did charitable works. He was referred to, respectfully, as 'the Major' by the local people, who would see him gliding by in his chauffeur-driven car. But he walked, every Sunday, to the church where his grave would be.

He said: 'Do you know what my father said to me, just before he died? He said, "I'm proud of you, Bob." And do you know what he meant by that? He meant I was a damn good mascot. I was the best bloody advertisement BMC ever had. He might have thought once I was a fool and a liability, but now – everything else apart – I was a walking asset. I'd be damn good for business.'

Every so often, I look through Dad's arms. Did you know that? He left them to me. Never threw one away. I live in this cottage in Wiltshire with a stash of nine artificial arms. All there. Except one, of course.

When Jenny said, 'What's in that big trunk?', I said, 'My father.' I didn't mean it as a bad joke.

You remember how he made such a thing of it? How it was a big day when he got a new model – when he 'went electronic'. How he used to talk about 'going to see his tailor'. And all those tired, old, obvious puns about being in the arms business.

I always wondered which way round it was: was he trying to make his arm like the rest of himself, or the rest of himself like his arm? I never saw the stump. What about you, Sophie? Never 'helped him in'. You never believed he was a different man once – before Anna, before you. I can't remember when I first thought: Dad has only one real arm – once he must have had two.

Another woman might have said: Jesus! Either they go or I do. Jenny said, 'Show me.'

Sometimes I've thought there must be some institution, some worthy cause somewhere that would be glad of them, that would know what to do with them. But then I've thought: These are bits of Dad.

They are like a miniature museum of prosthetic technology.

199

(The words we might never have had to learn!) But they are more than that. The earlier ones are shapely, useless bits of sculpture that gradually lose their anthropomorphic wishfulness and their aesthetic pretensions; the later ones look like nothing human, but actually simulate the function of an arm.

They are like an index of the twentieth century.

SOPHIE

———

You think it's a long time to be on a plane? Another six hours. You think they should get you from New York to London in – well, you tell me, how long? One hour? Half an hour? A couple of minutes?

But look at it another way. *Only* seven hours to fly from New York to London. It takes days to cross the Atlantic Ocean by ship. It used to take weeks. And once they didn't even know that America was *there*, on the other side. You're not impressed? You don't think it's so great to be thousands of feet up in the sky in a jumbo jet? You've done it before when we flew that time to Miami with Daddy. With Daddy. So what's new?

Or look at it another way. Seven hours. And yet we're flying so fast that we'll actually *shorten* time. You'll see. In a little while it'll be dark, but it won't stay dark for very long. Not like a normal night. When we land in London it'll be breakfast-time there, when for us it should still be the middle of the night. And it will all seem strange.

It's because we're travelling in one direction but the sun is travelling in another. And the sun is moving slower than we are. Don't you think that's wonderful? To be moving faster than the sun? Of course, it's not that the sun is *really* moving. The sun isn't really going anywhere. It's that the earth – It's –

When do they show us the movie? Oh, in a little while yet, I guess. When everyone's settled. First they give us a drink and some food on a tray. But you don't really want to watch the movie, do you? On planes it's always a bad movie. And don't you think it's *weird* – to be thousands of feet up in the air and to want to pretend you're in a movie-house? The real movie is out *there*, isn't it? Those clouds – look, we're *above* them! A whole ocean sliding underneath us.

You know, a long time ago, they'd have thought what we're doing now was magic. Impossible! Out of this world! They'd have thought only gods could fly up into the sky. And now we get into these things and stow our luggage and fasten our seat-belts – and say: How about something to keep us amused?!

Let's not watch the movie, my angels. Let's not even listen to the music on the head-sets. Don't neglect your mother. You know, I'm getting the feeling she's not such a good flier as you are. It's true, she's always been a little nervous. Ever since – Let's just be together, here, above the world. There are more important things than movies. And it'll be tomorrow sooner than you think. It'll be tomorrow before it's even stopped being today. And your mother has only six hours.

HARRY

—

But once everything was black and white. No, I don't mean simpler, clearer – when were they ever that? I mean, literally: monochrome.

Picture your father, Sophie, walking down Fleet Street on a grey, wet day in the grey post-war year of 1948. He wears the non-colours that are everywhere around him (like a true news photographer, he blends in with his surroundings): grey raincoat, dark suit, dark-grey trilby. The cars that pass him are black and grey. The city buildings are charcoal studies: soot and stone. The wet road and the clock-face over the *Daily Telegraph* building and the smoke from a train on the Black-friars line and the grey dome of St Paul's against a grey sky are all the tones of newsprint and photographs.

And yet his heart is full of colour, his heart is aglow with colour, in that year of your birth. More colour than it will ever have in the days of Kodachrome and technicolour and colour TVs and that mainstay of his future career, the Sunday colour supplement.

If you are happy, why go looking for trouble?

Colour appeared, in shy, unstable tints, in the Forties and Fifties, then blossomed – yellow cars! Pink shirts! Shop-fronts that fluoresced! – in that bright new age in which you grew up. Was all that to do with the perfecting of the three-colour emulsion process – as if the world had glimpsed itself in some new and flattering mirror – or was it to do, like rising hemlines and marijuana and rockets into space, with sheer high spirits? And was it only coincidence that the years that had preceded, the years of world wars and depressions and newsreels and family albums, should be clad, or so it seems in my memory, in sullen shades of grey?

Before there was colour there was black and white. But before there was black and white there was sepia, ochre, tawny, bronze. I was born – just about – in the age of sepia. And it has always seemed to me that before this black-and-white then technicolour century came of age, the world was brown. My father's world was brown. The brown of leather and horse-flesh and mahogany sideboards. The brown of old brown shires and rutted lanes before the spread of tar. Even the first cameras were little brown boxes, glossy and venerable as violins.

My father's desk was polished oak. And the study was oak panelled, and the spines of Uncle Edward's books were mostly brown, and even the plaster busts on the mantelpiece – Homer? Cicero? I forget – turning on me their blind eyes that brown afternoon, had acquired a faint, tobaccoey sheen.

The desk was unlocked – for once, negligently unlocked – and when I took from the top left-hand drawer that single sepia photograph, that colour brown, most familiar and companionable of colours, became all at once foreign and strange, the colour of things lost.

She is standing in front of some porch or verandah, in a long dress with a tight waist. And though the photographer was plainly no professional (but I knew that), you must give him his due. She is clutching in one hand a wide-brimmed summer hat which would have cast her face into deep shade were it on her head. The photographer has told her to take off the hat, and she has only just removed it. Her hair is slightly disarranged. She is trying to hold a pose, but it is clear that – because the photographer has not given her time or because of something he has said – it has slipped. Her eyes are wide in happy surprise, her lips are just parted.

Fact or phantom? Truth or mirage? I used to believe – to profess, in my professional days – that a photo is truth positive, fact incarnate and incontrovertible. And yet: explain to me that glimpse into unreality.

How can it be? How can it be that an instant which occurs once and once only, remains permanently visible? How could it be that a woman whom I had never known or seen before – though I had no doubt who she was – could be staring up at me from the brown surface of a piece of paper?

From a time before I existed. From a time before, perhaps, she had even thought of me and when she was undoubtedly ignorant of what I would mean to her.

I was nine years old. It was half-term. November 1927. Through the window – when I dared risk being seen myself – I could see him standing in a corner of the orchard, talking to the gardener (Davis?) who was prodding with a rake a sullenly burning heap of leaves. He is not yet thirty, but he has the bearing of a gruff, grizzled dignitary. He would surely have thrashed me – a fierce, left-handed thrashing – if he had known I had seen that photograph. Just as he would have chastised himself if he had known he had forgotten to lock his desk. As he had never forgotten, not for a single day in nine years, to lock up himself.

I put the photograph carefully back in the drawer, not daring to pry further. There was no way I could ask to look at it again without disclosing I had looked already. No way of knowing if that drawer would ever be left unlocked again.

Why locked away? Till I was fifteen years old and summoned the nerve to ask him, he never told me where she was buried.

205

The leaves on the trees in the orchard, like the leaves on the bonfire, were brown, and even the thick, reluctant smoke, trailing across a background of brown woodland, had an amber tinge to it. So that that scene, framed in the study window, was almost, itself, like an old, lost photograph. My father, caught unawares, as if I had him squarely in my sights. Talking to the gardener. Stepping back to avoid coils of autumnal smoke.

That Christmas I asked for a camera. Four years later he bought me one.

When I was ten years old, the following autumn, he took me on an aeroplane for a weekend in France. We could have gone by the traditional method, train and boat, but I know now that trains, which always evoke for me mournful journeys to and from boarding school, must have evoked for him even more mournful journeys – out of Waterloo to Southampton, and then again on the French side. Entrainings. Detrainings. Pass and warrant. So, in 1928, apart from reasons of ostentation and novelty, we flew. From Croydon to a military airfield somewhere north of Paris, in a specially chartered Armstrong-Whitworth Argosy, a monstrous, vibrant biplane, with an open cockpit, three engines, fifteen or so other passengers and a cabin interior which would now seem both absurdly plush and prehistoric.

Perhaps that aeroplane trip was only a bribe for my good behaviour in the days that immediately followed. We were there to mark the ten-year-old Armistice, and somehow a public truce had to descend on our own ten-year enmity. I had to play the dutiful and admiring son of my good soldier father. The bribe must have been effective. The Armistice meant nothing to me. And being in a foreign country for the first time was nothing to being several thousand feet up in the air, from where, in fact, one country looked much like another and the demarcations of maps and atlases seemed suddenly a sham.

I wish I could remember more of those three days in France:

a turreted, mansarded French hotel; an old French matron, with a distinct moustache, who must have been employed to look after the children of wealthier guests; many men, like my father, wearing dark coats and medals; an occasion in a big square before a cathedral, with bugles and rain; drives to some inexplicable places in the middle of muddy fields (there was much talk about mud – 'the mud'). And a sense, yes, in spite of myself, that he was pleased with me, and I, in return, was perversely proud of him, that in that strange, ceremonial and rigid atmosphere he was actually unfreezing and making some sort of bid to be like a man I might know. Had I been older I might have thought: Is it possible, is it possible, then? That he means to come out of mourning?

In the evenings a little hotel band would strike up its medley of what must have been mildly jazzed up versions of old trench songs. He watched the dancing like some old buffer tolerating the ways of a frivolous young world.

I don't even remember the name of the hotel. Or the names of those places we drove to in the rain. My thoughts were on that astonishing aerial journey and the equally astonishing one we would have to make back. And he must have somehow appreciated this. As we waited to board for the return trip, he slipped away momentarily and reappeared with the hint of a gleam in his eye which was not, for once, a piece of public play-acting but a genuine, faltering attempt at fatherliness. I don't know where this fondness came from, but it seems, as I recall it, that there was something valedictory about it, as if he knew, even then, how the gap between us would only widen further.

A moment later a steward, with a knowing look, ushered us through a doorway, and we followed him across the tarmac to the waiting plane. Standing by its ponderous, uptilted fuselage and dressed in the outlandish costume, goggles and all, which was then *de rigueur* for airline crew, was no less a person than the pilot. And in no time, while Dad waited below, this same fancy-dress pilot had somehow whisked me up behind the huge, bristling, forward engine and sat me down amidst an array of instruments which would now seem impossibly archaic but which seemed to me then like the very stuff of the future.

I was entranced, Sophie. Entranced.

Perched beside that pilot in that ancient Argosy, I almost forgot my father standing beneath us on the tarmac. It was as if he had pushed me forward into this wondrous outlook on the sky, had made me a present of it, then discreetly withdrawn. I might soar away; he would remain. And though he had staged it all (slipping a coin into the steward's hand: Yes, of course, no trouble, no trouble at all for Major Beech, v.c.), perhaps he was aware, himself, of being only half present. I can see now that throughout that homeward journey his feet must have been, so to speak, still on the ground, still caught in the mud. And I was being lifted up and away, out of his world, out of the age of mud, out of that brown, obscure age, into the age of air.